SUFFRAGETTE

My Story.

SUFFRAGETTE

The Diary of
Dollie Baxter, London 1909-1913

By Carol Drinkwater

SCHOLASTIC

In loving memory of a dear friend and a fine
and generous woman, Dr Jill Wolff

While the events described and some of the characters in this book may be
based on actual historical events and real people, Dollie Baxter is a fictional
character, created by the author, and her diary is a work of fiction.

My thanks as always to my editors at Scholastic, Susila Baybars and Jill Sawyer

Scholastic Children's Books
Commonwealth House, 1–19 New Oxford Street,
London, WC1A 1NU, UK
A division of Scholastic Ltd
London ~ New York ~ Toronto ~ Sydney ~ Auckland
Mexico City ~ New Delhi ~ Hong Kong

Published in the UK by Scholastic Ltd, 2003

Text copyright © Carol Drinkwater, 2003

ISBN 0 439 98268 5

London

28th March 1909

Lady Violet Campbell, the owner of this Georgian manor house in the depths of the Gloucestershire countryside, was buried today in the cemetery of the church at Dymock. Lady Violet, whom I loved with all my heart, died peacefully in her sleep six days ago after a short illness.

Many of her family and friends travelled up from London yesterday to be here for the service this morning, and tonight the house is packed to the rafters with sleeping people. Most of them know nothing of my existence and I am keeping myself well hidden.

I made my way here by train from Cheltenham to pay my respects. Charlton Kings is where I live during the week. I lodge with a kind-hearted family who were chosen by the late Lady Violet to look after me during school term. I could have boarded at my school, the Cheltenham Ladies' College, but Lady Violet decided that it would be better for me to share the company of a family.

"Because you have lost your own, dear," she reasoned.

You would assume from reading this that I am from a wealthy family, that I was born into the upper class, known here in England as the privileged class, but that is not at all the case.

My name is Dollie Baxter. I am fourteen-and-a-half years old, and I am the only daughter of a working-class man, John Baxter, who spent all his life labouring for a pittance at Bonningtons, one of the two biggest dockyard companies in London. But my father, who was a stevedore by profession, has been dead these past four years. I was ten years old when he passed away and his leaving us changed my life more than I could ever have dreamed was possible. I was uprooted and, quite literally, furnished with a new existence. All that was left of my past were my memories and my name.

So you see, I am a working-class girl of no means, and the knowledge of this fact might better explain my plight now that dear Lady Violet has passed away.

My mother is illiterate. Not a single syllable can she read or write, and nor does she have employment. The opportunities were never made available to her. Still, in a roundabout way, it is due to her illiteracy that I have been given this new life, this splendid opportunity. When my father died she was grieving and almost destitute. The only path open to her was to give me away. Lady Violet offered to take me, in a manner of speaking, and, eventually, my mother accepted.

I have four brothers, all of whom are older than I am. I never see them because they live in the same area as my mother in the East End of London. They have followed in my father's footsteps and are all employed at the Bonnington dockyards. I suspect that they disapprove of this gift of education that has been settled on me. Perhaps they blame my mother for what she did? Who can say? I cannot answer because I don't know. The important thing for me is that I don't blame her. I firmly believe that she judged it to be the best course open to me and, in any case, she had no real choice.

Lord, I am exhausted. All these memories are distressing. But if I don't write about my situation how else will I ever come to terms with it? I have no one now. I am alone and must find a way to fend for myself. That is the reason for this diary. I shall use it, these blank pages, as I would a friend, a kindly ear, as Lady Violet has always been for me.

There's someone knocking at the door! I'd better stop writing and turn down the gaslight. I will continue later or tomorrow.

Later, almost midnight

That knock gave me quite a fright, but I had no reason to worry. It was Rachel and Sarah. They work in the kitchens here and were bringing me a tray of food. They knew that I had not eaten since before I set off this morning. I could not be more grateful for their kindnesses. They made up this room for me and welcomed me as the regular visitor I have always been to this house. Of course on previous occasions I had my own suite of rooms and tonight I am up in the staff quarters, but that doesn't really bother me.

Rachel and Sarah sprawled on the bed and chatted while I devoured my vegetable soup and roast chicken. I was ravenous.

"Who's stayed over?" I asked.

"The whole bloomin' family," replied Sarah.

"Lady Flora, too?"

"She's in the room beneath. What a beauty she is. Slender as a stalk of hay." This was Rachel, who always worries that she is fat and plain and will never find a husband. "Are you going to introduce yourself to her, Dollie?"

I shrugged. "Not yet. It's too soon."

"What are you going to do then?"

"I don't know," I answered.

"Don't none of them know about you?"

I shook my head.

"Same boat as us you're in then. Out on a limb. We don't know if we'll have jobs this time next week."

"Whoever inherits this house will keep you on. Cook will speak up for you both," I assured them. "I'd help you, if only I could."

They wished me goodnight and we all expressed the desire to meet again before too long when, I hope, all our circumstances will have improved.

They will find positions, no doubt about it. My own situation is more awkward and I have no idea how it will be resolved. You see, I was Lady Violet's secret.

29th March 1909, before dawn

In spite of tiredness, I cannot sleep, so I shall write on.

Yesterday morning I was in a real sweat. I was running late because my journey took longer than I had anticipated. Starting out from Cheltenham, I was obliged to change trains in Gloucester. Unfortunately my first train was delayed, so I missed my connection and had to hang about for the next one. Once aboard I settled to the journey. It was a beautiful morning. Everywhere the fields were carpeted with daffodils. Staring out at the rolling green hillsides, the fresh spring growth, the orchards in bud, ponds with ducks and clear streams with men on the banks fishing for trout, I was marvelling at the sharpness of life beyond the carriage window, while I was en route to say my farewells to the woman who has lavished more generosity on me than any other. As my train drew closer to its destination, I spied the steeples of the neighbouring parishes, all of which I have explored many times so I know their streets and leafy lanes by heart. It's a glorious sight, I said to myself as the train steamed along. I shall miss it all horribly.

Upon arrival at Dymock, I hared up the hill, muttering crossly to myself about not having taken the dawn train. By the time I reached the village church, which is set back from the road and hidden behind spreading chestnuts and a splendid yew tree, the service was already under way. Try as I might I could not squeeze my way in. It was jam-packed. The crowds were spilling out of the great Norman doorway, pressed up tight against one another on the gravelled path, straining to hear the sermon. Finally I gave up, stepped away from the path and settled on the grass beneath a chestnut tree adorned with sticky buds.

Once the service was over, groups of people began to make their way across the cemetery to the graveside, where the sight of freshly dug earth heaped high made my stomach tight. There must have been more than 400 present. I held back, not only because I had arrived late and felt ashamed for it, but because there were so many faces I wanted to see in the flesh for the first time and because my emotions were at sixes and sevens. What would be my role in this county of Gloucestershire after today? Would I ever set eyes on this place again? I speculated. Who, if I had stepped forward and announced myself, would have opened their arms to accept me as a Bonnington?

Many of the Bonnington clan, as well as the staff from their family house in Cadogan Square in London – all great admirers of Lady Violet – were present. I recognized Flora the instant I set eyes on her.

Well, it was not so difficult. Her picture has frequently appeared in newspapers due to her activities as a prominent suffragist and because she is carving a career for herself in the modern industry of the art of the motion picture. Also her grandmother, Lady Violet, kept dozens of photographs of her all over the house. There's a stunning one on the grand piano in the music room. She spoke of her favourite granddaughter endlessly and with enormous affection and pride. Sometimes it made me quite jealous.

So even though I was seeing Flora for the first time, I felt as though I already knew her. I watched her intently, scrutinizing her. She is every bit as lovely as the world says. How I longed to move up close but, sensitive to her loss and grieving, I kept my distance.

Flora was accompanied by two young men, both of whom are writers and applauded for their poetry: Rupert Brooke and John Drinkwater. Each of them has a small house only a few miles distant from the village of Dymock and they were frequent guests at Lady Violet's dinner parties. I stepped back into the shade as the trio, deep in subdued conversation, passed by. It was not that I wished to avoid them. On the contrary, they are both fascinating company, but I was not prepared in that moment to be introduced to Flora. It was not the right occasion.

Following behind were Mrs Millicent Fawcett and her equally celebrated sister, Dr Elizabeth Garrett Anderson. Both visited the house during my years there and I was presented to them, but only for split seconds. They worked and campaigned alongside Lady Violet. They are suffragists. In fact, Mrs Fawcett is a very famous name in the fight for women's votes. I have many newspaper cuttings about her and her sister in my suffrage scrapbook.

The Bonnington family and friends encircled the graveside. I easily recognized Henrietta, Flora's older sister, and her husband, Viscount Marsh. He was born in this county – his family own vast acres of arable farmland here – and he and Henrietta met at Lady Violet's many years ago. Their two small sons flanked them. They were also in the company of an elderly, stooped gentleman with grey hair and moustache. I felt my heart race and my blood boil as I stared hard at his face, at his impassive features. Sir Thomas Bonnington, Lady Violet's son-in-law, founder of the

Bonnington dockyard empire and my mother's enemy. How she hated him! The accursed man who, she claimed, drove my poor father "to an early grave".

If I stepped forward and announced myself, would the name Baxter mean anything at all to him? That was what I was asking myself when, all of a sudden, as the vicar was on the point of a prayer, a hush descended even more awesome than the reverence of mourning. A late-arriving carriage had drawn up and out stepped a very stylish woman in her early fifties, dressed in black satin – Mrs Emmeline Pankhurst, the leading figure in the fight for women's votes. She strode purposefully along the stone pathway. I turned quickly to observe the crowd gathered round the graveside. Many eyes were upon her. Wherever she goes Mrs Pankhurst is greeted with a mixed response. There are those who are full of admiration for her work, for her charismatic manner and her courage and, above all, for the way in which she energizes women of all ages and class to join her cause. Then there are those – and I caught sight of a few of them yesterday morning – who despise her for what she does, for the fact that she, a respectable and well-bred woman, was imprisoned twice last year.

"We are here not because we are law-breakers; we are here in our efforts to become law-makers." These were her last words to the magistrate at her trial before he found her guilty and ordered her to keep the peace for twelve months or spend three months in Holloway. She chose prison, saying that she would never keep the peace until women were given the same voting rights as men.

Yesterday, Mrs Pankhurst ignored the reactions of the mourners. Instead, she made her way proudly towards Flora and positioned herself like an older, caring sister, behind her.

To see her standing there, not 50 yards away from me, made my heart quicken. She is a heroine to me. Lady Violet has talked to me on many occasions about the history of the women's movement and the directions the struggle is taking, but I still have much to learn. One day soon, I intend to join them in their fight. Their cause will be my cause! It is already in my heart.

As the coffin was lowered into the ground and the mourners, led by the vicar, recited the final prayer, I kept my distance and my face in shadow. Several local people spied me and nodded to me, but the family paid me no attention. If any had raised their bowed heads and glanced in my direction, they would probably have taken me for a local girl who worked as a kitchen maid up at the manor house. Not in their wildest imaginings could they have guessed what my place in the life of this lady had been.

Once the funeral was over, the crowds began making their way in dribs and drabs through the noon-day sunshine to the carriages and motor cars awaiting them beyond the lych-gate at the end of the stone pathway. I hung back until the cemetery had emptied. I wanted the opportunity to say a private and heartfelt thank you to the woman closed within that coffin.

I stayed a while, kneeling on the grass, talking to Lady Violet as though she were present and listening to all that I was confiding to her. I could picture her grey-haired head, tilted sideways, her deep-blue eyes. It was the way she always looked when she was concentrating. No matter how occupied she was, she always found time for me.

Afterwards, I made my way on foot to the manor house, trudging slowly to the servants' entrance where I knew I would find a welcome. Agnes, the cook, promised to send up a square meal after the guests had all been fed, and Sarah and Rachel hurried away to find clean sheets.

So, here I am, bereft in this attic room. I shall stop writing now and try to get some sleep because I must take a train back to Cheltenham later this morning.

1st April 1909

I am back at school, but I don't want to be here any more. I keep thinking about my family. But I can never go back. I promised my mother she'd never see me again. I feel lost, rootless. I want to run away. Perhaps I should change my name, make my way to London and join the Women's Social and Political Union (the WSPU).

I copied a newspaper article pinned to the bulletin board this evening. It reported that twelve female suffrage demonstrators were arrested outside the House of Commons yesterday. What must it feel like to be arrested?

My English teacher, Mrs Bertram, was not at all cross that I had not written my essay for this afternoon's class. She is usually so strict, but all she said was, "The end of the week will be fine." Mrs Partridge, our headmistress, must have told her about Lady Violet.

19th April 1909

I was searching through *The Times* in the library during break this morning when I spotted an article reporting that Mrs Emmeline Pethwick-Lawrence, the treasurer of the WSPU and a personal friend of Emmeline Pankhurst, was released from Holloway prison three days ago after serving a two-month sentence. One thousand supporters were waiting at the gates to cheer her as she walked to freedom. What a splendid moment that must have been. How I would have loved to have been there.

I was about to copy the details into my scrapbook when Miss Manners, the librarian, leaned over. "You have a visitor," she whispered. "Come with me."

I was surprised because I had not been expecting anyone.

She led me to the waiting rooms that adjoin our headmistress's offices and instructed me to wait. About five minutes later, the door reopened and in walked Mrs Partridge followed by Lady Flora! I was amazed.

"Stand up please, Dollie," said Mrs Partridge. "I want to introduce you to Lady Flora Bonnington. She has travelled up from London to speak to you. I shall leave you with her. Remember to deport yourself in the manner of a young lady who is both educated and respectfully modest."

I nodded, and with that we were left alone. I felt awkward and shy, yet thrilled to be standing there with Flora. She stepped forward and brushed her elegant fingers lightly against my cheek.

"Do feel at ease, Dollie. There is no need for us to be formal with one another." She sat as she spoke and gestured to me to follow suit, which I did. "Do you have any idea why I am here?"

I panicked, tongue-tied. I had no notion what she might have learned of me, or what I was expected to answer. So I made no response besides a shrug.

"I think the name of my grandmother, Lady Violet Campbell, means something to you, does it not?"

"But of course," I stammered.

"You were her ward, isn't that so?"

"Yes, I ... I was." I felt the tears welling up in my eyes. Was she here to inform me that I must leave the school? I would not have minded now that Lady Violet was no longer in Gloucestershire, but where was I to go?

"Mrs Partridge tells me that my grandmother was the one who placed you at this school. She says that you are a hardworking and very gifted student and that you have ambitions to become a journalist. Is that true?"

I nodded.

"Splendid. I also gather that you requested two days' absence from school to attend Lady Violet's funeral. Were you there?"

Again I nodded.

"I am sorry that you did not make yourself known to me or to another member of my family."

"I wanted to, but I didn't feel that it was correct to intrude."

At this, Flora smiled. "Forgive my asking, Dollie, but are you an orphan?"

"No. Well, not exactly. My father died a few years ago but my mother, as far as I know, is still living."

My answer seemed to confuse her. She frowned, fathoming the puzzle – if I had a mother why did I need a guardian?

"This was among my grandmother's papers," she said. She fished into her velvet handbag and pulled out an official-looking document. "It is a letter, hand written by her to her solicitor, Mr Makepeace, giving clear and precise instructions for your future."

I felt my stomach tighten and the palms of my hands go sticky.

"My grandmother has set aside sufficient funds from her estate for your board and keep and for your education through to and including university, if that is where your ambitions lie. She mentions that her personal preference would be for you to attend St Hilda's College at Oxford but she states that you must be free to choose and to follow whatever path you believe is yours. She has also requested that the sum of two thousand pounds be invested for you. You are to inherit this sum plus the monies that it will have accrued on your 21st birthday."

I was dumbfounded. I have never had one penny of my own and the very idea that Lady Violet would think of me in her last moments left me speechless. More embarrassingly, it reduced me to tears.

Sitting there, just a few feet away from Flora, I bowed my head, desperate to hide the rush of tears rolling down my cheeks. I was crying for the unexpected generosity shown to me by someone who had already been so kind to me and because I'd lost her. In all these weeks since I had been told of her passing away, it was the first time I had allowed my emotions to express themselves. I sniffled an apology for my foolishness and dug about in my pockets for a handkerchief. Flora offered me hers, a lacy one, then waited while I regained my composure.

"May I ask how you first came to know my grandmother?" she eventually inquired and with warmth. She didn't seem to be the least bit put out that a healthy sum of what should have been her and her sister's inheritance had been willed to me.

"She came to our cottage," I muttered. "My father was not there. He was out with my four brothers. They were marching with the strikers. Being a girl and the youngest, I was home with Mother. I cannot remember the exchange that took place between Lady Campbell and my mother during that first visit, though I stayed close to my mother's knee throughout their interview. I was only five at the time. What I do recall, though, is how she smelt."

"Whatever do you mean by that?" exclaimed Flora.

"She smelt so sweet. Of eau de Cologne. Perfumes and scented waters were all quite unknown to me then. In our neighbourhood, other less pleasant odours mingled and filled the air. But your grandmother did not seem to be disgusted or shocked."

"Disgusted by what?" asked Flora. It was evident from her questions that she had never visited areas of London where the very poor live.

"Well, her graceful manners and the finery of her clothes were quite at odds with the surroundings in which she found herself. She wore leather gloves and a hat decorated with glorious purple plumes and she had arrived in a motor car. It was driven by a man in goggles who stepped out to open the door for her and draw off the blanket that was covering her; a protection against the wind, I suppose. Her arrival remains vivid to me even to this day because I had never seen a motor car before. It was autumn and the air was chilly. She bent to ask a group of children playing in the cobbled lane which cottage was ours. They stared, stupefied, and then I saw one of them point with filthy fingers towards our open door. Your grandmother thanked them with a bag of boiled sweets."

"Have you any idea what prompted her to pay you a visit?"

I hesitated. I feared my answer might offend Flora.

"It seems that my mother had turned up unannounced and uninvited at your family home in Cadogan Square and had made a rumpus at the door. She can get very riled sometimes and I remember that she was spoiling for a fight on that day."

"Really? Why?"

25

"She had been determined to see Thomas Bonnington, who, she was informed, was not at home."

"Whatever would she have wanted with my father?"

"It was during the dockers' strike of 1900. We had no money. My mother was angry but, more importantly, she was frightened and desperate, worrying how to feed us children and pay our rent. I don't know how your grandmother came to hear about my mother's visit to your house, but she did. She came, she said, because she was concerned for our welfare. She offered help, but my mother sent her packing. Mother said we weren't in need of charity and certainly not from a member of the Bonnington family."

As I recounted this incident of almost a decade earlier, I caught my breath. Flora's father had brought so much misery and hardship upon my family. Still, I have never held Flora responsible and was about to say so, but she interrupted me.

"Baxter, of course! Dollie *Baxter*! How foolish of me not to have made the connection earlier. Your mother is Mrs Baxter. Good Lord, yes! I remember her visit to our home very well indeed. I remember her, too. And, yes, your father is a docker, employed by my father and—"

"He's been dead these past four years."

"I'm sorry. Yes, you told me that. Please go on with your story and forgive my interruption."

"In spite of my mother's rejection, your grandmother came back to visit us from time to time, over many years. She talked to my mother, asked her questions, listened to what she had to say. It was suggested that she would like to see me educated. I was the youngest and the only daughter. I couldn't go to work on the docks. Lady Campbell painted a picture of a life for me that my mother could never have dreamed of. 'Think of it, Mrs Baxter,' she said, 'if Dollie could read and write and in due course earn her own living, it would give her the opportunity to become an independent woman.'

"What your grandmother was saying rang true, but my mother was defensive. She refused outright and with harsh words. 'We don't need your kind here,' she declared. As far as I know she never discussed it with my father and I am not sure she ever really comprehended why your grandmother would want to waste her resources on a family like ours. 'Working class, that's what we are, Dollie. The bottom of the heap,' she used to say to me. 'Derided by the rest of society.' But at some point she began to trust Lady Campbell and little by little came round to the idea.

'And there's precious little future on offer for you elsewhere,' she'd mutter. It was as though she was trying to convince herself that she was making the right decision. But it wasn't until I turned ten, a short while after the death of my father, that my mother finally made up her mind.

"She woke one morning full of resolution. 'Come along, miss,' she announced. We walked for miles, looking out for a place where she could telephone to ask Lady Campbell to drop by. When your grandmother arrived a few days later, my mother explained her predicament – that she had recently lost her husband and was penniless save for the sums two of her sons brought home (my other brothers had married and left by then). She feared ending her days in the poorhouse and had come to realize that here was an opportunity for me to have a better life.

"'I'm doing this for you, Dollie,' she said the evening before I was due to leave. 'I want you to have a future. God knows, I don't want you to end up like me.'

"The following morning we said our goodbyes. I watched her struggling with her emotions and hugged her so tight. 'I'll come back soon,' I whispered, choked with my own.

"'No, you won't,' she barked. 'Forget me. Forget all this. I don't want to see your face here again. Promise me you'll never return.'

"'But…'

"'Promise, Dollie.'

"I nodded, failing hopelessly to fight off tears."

"What happened then?" asked Flora.

"I was driven in a chauffeured motor car to Paddington Station, given a ticket and put on a train to Gloucestershire. It was the first time I had ridden in a train. I was headed for your grandmother's estate. When we arrived at the country station where I had been instructed to get off, a porter met me. I remember how puzzled he was that I had no luggage, no belongings of any sort. He hailed a horse-drawn cab and within the hour I was with your grandmother."

"But how absolutely extraordinary that she never mentioned a word about you or any of this story to me," mused Flora.

"I have often wondered why she bothered with me, but on the few occasions when I begged her to tell me she fobbed me off without giving me a satisfactory explanation."

"I think I might know the answer," said Flora.

"Really? What is it?"

"Let's leave it for another day, but I will tell you when the time is right. Meanwhile, please, tell me all about your life at this famous school. Are you happy here?"

"I am very fortunate, though I am a bit of a square peg in a round hole."

"I don't follow."

"I'm the only girl of working-class origins here."

"Ah, I see. Yes, that could be difficult. How long have you been here?"

"Two years. Before that, while I was at living at your grandmother's, I was tutored by a governess. I couldn't read or write when I left home. There was a lot to learn. I had to work very hard. Then I attended a school in one of the neighbouring country towns for a short while and only later, when it was agreed that I would be able to keep up, was I enrolled here. But, in answer to your question, yes, I was happy here until Lady Campbell died, but now I feel…"

"What?"

"Cut off. Alone. For the first time since I arrived in Gloucestershire, I am really homesick. I long to return to the city."

Flora rose, took me in her arms and embraced me like a sister. "You are never again to consider yourself alone. I am certain, Dollie, that you and I will become the best of friends. My grandmother's wish is that I replace her as your guardian. On a temporary basis, at least, until you and circumstances choose us another direction. What do you say to that? I realize that we are as yet barely acquainted, but I would like you to think of me as a sister, or if you feel that I am too old for such a role then how about a kindly aunt?"

"Sisters!" I exclaimed. "Oh, yes, please."

"And how would you like to come and stay with me for a few days at my house in London? We could organize it for May."

I was overwhelmed. Such a generous offer was unexpected.

"What do you say, Dollie?"

"I would love it," I answered shyly.

"Then it's settled. I shall speak to Mrs Partridge and arrange everything."

"Thank you. Thank you so much."

We said our goodbyes and I hurried back to the library, where I had left my books. I was horribly late for maths, but I didn't care. I could hardly believe my good fortune. It was as though all that I had been longing for was suddenly being offered to me.

17th May 1909

Flora's home is in Bloomsbury, a district of London slightly north-west of the city centre. A horse-drawn cab awaited me as I came out of the station at Paddington the day before yesterday. It delivered me right to her door. She was waiting there with open arms to greet me, and since then I have not found a single minute to write my diary until now.

I have never visited such a place before. It is a tall, narrow house in a terraced row. There are five storeys, and my room is on the fourth. The place is spilling over with visitors and guests. I feel SO SHY. But what a splendidly lively environment! Each room is chock-a-block with fine furniture and furnishings, including Art Nouveau lamps and chairs and goodness knows what else. (I had never heard of Art Nouveau until Flora showed me some examples.) The dining table is carved mahogany and has twelve matching chairs. The curtains are of a printed fabric from a famous department store in Regent Street, Liberty's.

Writers, designers and film-makers are endlessly around. Almost all of them are from Europe or America. One or two of them are staying here, while the rest drop by to discuss their ideas or to be introduced to like-minded artists. Flora says that she sees her home as a focal point for creative thinkers. It is all dazzlingly bohemian.

Every room I enter, I discover gaggles of artistic folk bawling good-naturedly in an assortment of languages. French seems to be their common ground, not English, while Flora skips easily from one to the other. Yesterday, she introduced me to two French film-makers: Alice Guy, a highly regarded director who taught Flora in Paris, and Max Linder, a dapper, internationally famous actor and director. Cecil Hepworth, a British producer, was also present.

"Has anyone seen his new picture, *The Lonely Villa*? You must! You simply must!" Hepworth was shouting, while waving his arms to emphasize his point. "It's a magnificent example of intercutting, Alice! And what drama his techniques create!"

His comrades were deep in debate. It transpired that their passionate exchange was about an American director called DW Griffith who, Alice explained to me, is revolutionizing the technical language of motion pictures. "Intercutting", "close-up figures". I did not understand these terms because I have never seen a motion picture, but I didn't own up to it.

France, someone claimed, continues to be the most important film-producing country in the world, and its film business is rapidly expanding. Another woman, an American with a necklace of large amber beads and smoking a cigarette, disagreed loudly. She claimed American Biograph was the most innovative film company in the world.

Flora spoke of her high hopes for England. "And what of London? It is the financial centre of the world, but I dream of giving it equal status as an artistic centre. I want to live in an England where women's rights and talents are recognized and thoroughly exercised. Today, there is not one woman working as a director of films here, but I intend to change that."

Lord, I was exhausted just listening to them. Such intensity and passion! Oh, I adore it here. There is much I shall learn and, for the first time in ages, I feel light-hearted.

18th May 1909

I slept for ever and woke late! I hadn't realized that I was so tired. There has been so much coming and going that I didn't notice until this morning, when the house was calm, that Flora has two truly gorgeous silver-blue cats. I found them curled up asleep on one of the Liberty chairs when I went in for breakfast.

19th May 1909

We had luncheon today with a journalist friend of Flora's who writes for the *Times Literary Supplement* and lives round the corner from here in Gordon Square. Her name is Virginia Stephen. She is a rather delicate-looking lady with wistful eyes and a pale face shaped like a long leaf. She and her sister, a painter called Vanessa Bell, along with several other friends of theirs, are the founders of a locally-based society known as the Bloomsbury Group. Flora is also a member. Among the other guests at lunch was a Labour politician from Scotland, Keir Hardie. He is a well-known supporter of the women's movement and a great friend of the Pankhursts.

"What does your group do?" I asked Miss Stephen. "What is its purpose?"

"We are all of us passionate about the arts and believe that the highest form of social progress is the accessibility of art to everyone. All society should be entitled to enjoy the pleasures of human intercourse and the enjoyment of beautiful objects."

I could not always follow the subject matters but the discussions were very lively. The talk was of social progress, sexual equality and the "strictures of the Victorian Age".

From time to time I nodded and tried to look intelligent. I agreed with much that was said, particularly about sexual equality, but I remained silent. I felt too shy to speak.

By then it was about time for tea. The others left and Flora invited me to her study. It smells of leather from the big chairs and the hundreds of books lining the shelves. I was glad everyone had gone because we had barely seen one another since I arrived.

"When I was your age, Dollie," she said, "one of my favourite pastimes was afternoon tea with Grandma. Cook would serve us my favourite home-made biscuits and then, once we were settled and I was tucking contentedly into the goodies, Grandma would encourage me to talk. She wanted to know all about my worries and my hopes and joys."

"Yes," I said. "She used to ask me the same."

"Do you intend to try for Oxford, as my grandmother obviously hoped for you?"

I do desire to go to university, but I did not have the confidence to say so. How could a working-class girl like me, even with the special opportunities that have been bestowed upon her, dare to count on the possibility of Oxford?

"I am very touched that Lady Campbell has made such a path available to me," was my response. "I will work hard and do my best."

"Have you decided what you will read if you are accepted there? Or do your imaginings take you travelling? Perhaps you fancy studying medicine or law?"

I hesitated. So many questions.

"What do you hope for, Dollie? What do you dream of achieving? Do tell, darling."

"I intend to be a journalist."

"Ah, yes, I had forgotten. And what will you use your pen to fight for?"

I was a bit sheepish about divulging any of my secret plans but eventually, because Flora continued to press me – "Tell me every detail and I will do my utmost to assist you." – I confided that I wanted to follow in the footsteps of Lady Violet, and of Flora herself. "Your grandmother always taught me that votes for women are essential, but that the vote is only the beginning. And that is what I feel, too."

"Indeed, Dollie, it is only the beginning. Once we have won the right to vote, we will have been given the opportunity to voice our opinions and to be heard throughout the Empire. We can make a difference."

"Do you believe that one day it will be possible to offer every woman the chance of a decent education? To give them self-respect and equal rights with men?"

"Yes! We will put women into Parliament, Dollie. Think of it. Women contributing to the way our country is governed. Women like my great friend Christabel Pankhurst. She has a degree in law and showed her skills with such brilliance when she defended both herself and her mother at their trial last year. But do you know that she is barred from practising her profession as a barrister for the simple reason that she is a woman? Her qualifications and talent, which are outstanding, count for nothing. When we have the vote such sexual injustices will be swept aside."

"England was the first country to grant women the right to practise medicine, wasn't it?"

"Yes," smiled Flora. "Yes, Dollie, it was."

"So why not law? Or politics? It doesn't make sense," I added.

Flora poured me another cup of tea and glanced across to the grand piano where a splendid silver-framed photograph of Lady Violet took pride of place. "My grandmother dedicated her life to the Votes for Women campaign and working for those less fortunate than herself," she continued. "As did my mother, I believe. Sexual equality was their goal, as it is mine. So you dream of being a suffragist, Dollie?"

"No, I intend to be a suffragette."

Flora stared at me quizzically. "A suffragette? Do you understand the difference between suffragists and suffragettes?"

"The *Daily Mail* christened the women fighting for votes 'suffragettes' and, like you and your grandmother, I want to wear that name honourably. You ask me what I dream of? Well, I want to fight, too. I want to see women such as my mother given the opportunity to learn to read and write, to be more than the domestic help in the home, to be treated decently, equally. Never to be…" I paused because I was about to touch upon a private matter that I am not ready to discuss, not even with Flora.

Flora sensed my reticence. "Never to be what, Dollie?" she interrogated.

"Never to be subjected to male dominance, never again to be at their beck and call. It is a question of human rights and, if necessary, I will give my life to the cause," I confided.

Flora laughed in a kindly way and suggested that perhaps I should not consider such dramatic resolutions. "I doubt that any of us will be called upon to give our lives, Dollie. At least, I sincerely hope that we won't."

I did not feel it polite to remind her that Mrs Pankhurst has described her organization as a "suffrage army fighting in the field" and so I kept quiet.

Flora promised to give me all the support she could. She explained, though, that she is with the constitutionalists not the militants. "We of the National Union of Women's Suffrage Societies, the NUWSS, are suffragists, Dollie, not suffragettes. We advocate legal means of campaigning such as parliamentary lobbying, whereas the more militant activists, those in the WSPU, the organization founded in 1903 by Emmeline and Christabel Pankhurst, are the women the *Daily Mail* dubbed 'suffragettes'. It was intended as an insult because they are judged unladylike and because they are willing to break the law to achieve their goals."

"Yes, I know that the WSPU is the more militant of the two leading suffrage organizations," I countered, for I didn't want Flora to believe me ignorant. "And I know exactly what first caused them to become more extreme," I added.

"Really?" she replied with surprise.

"On 19th May in 1905, a group of ten women went to speak to the Prime Minister. Amongst these women was 76-year-old Emily Davies who handed the women's suffrage petition to the Prime Minister. His answer to them was, 'Be patient.' This was not the response they had expected. Women (and some men) had been actively campaigning for votes for women since the 1860s and they were tired of being patient. And so the movement grew in momentum and it became militant."

"Well, yes, Dollie, that is one of the incidents that fired the desire to fight harder and more vehemently. But my way, the way of the NUWSS, headed by Millicent Garrett Fawcett, is equally active. We have the same burning ambition to see women enfranchised. Why not consider allying yourself with us?"

"But if both organizations are fighting the same battle...?"

"They are, but their approaches are different, and although Christabel and I have known one another since I was your age and she is a dear friend whom I admire, I do not always agree with the means she uses. And I think it is important you know that my grandmother was a suffragist. She was never a suffragette."

I was taken aback. I had always assumed that Lady Violet was a suffragette.

20th May 1909

This morning Flora took me shopping to buy clothes that she feels will better suit my needs here in London.

"But I am only staying ten days!" I exclaimed.

"Well, you can leave them in the wardrobe for your next visit," she laughed. "That blue bedroom is now exclusively yours."

We travelled to Knightsbridge in a hansom. This is a long, low vehicle that holds two passengers with a driver seated on a high deck behind. It was the first I had ever been in. Before being set down outside Harrods, a terrifyingly posh and shockingly expensive store, we made a short detour to Cadogan Square.

"My father lives there." Flora pointed to one of the tall, elegant houses.

I felt myself stiffen. "Are we going in?" I asked nervously.

"Another day, perhaps. I wanted you to see where your mother came during the dockers' strike. I was descending the stairs, I remember it clearly, and I saw her waiting at the door. I went to ask if I could help

43

her, but she refused point blank to deal with me. Eventually one of the staff turned her away.

"I think the reason my grandmother made the journey to the East End in search of you all was because I had told her about your mother's visit. The incident had troubled me greatly. I had not known what to do for the best. I brooded over it until, eventually, I turned to Grandma."

"And you think that your meeting my mother was what prompted Lady Campbell to visit our home and offer us assistance?"

Flora considered my question. "It was a part of the reason. And now see, Dollie, after all these years, here we are together like sisters. An odd turn of events, don't you agree?"

And I do agree. Still, I sensed that there was more to the story than Flora would tell. I love her already, though I am deeply conscious of our differences. We are poles apart! Even when we were looking at clothes today, I preferred the simpler, practical dresses, while Flora was excited by flamboyant and ornate gowns. But she did not insist and bought me those I chose.

After we returned from our shopping expedition and I had thanked her for my two new outfits – they are lovely – she promised that before I left she would take me to the Prince's Skating Rink, which is also in Knightsbridge, quite close to Harrods.

"But I can't skate."

"No, you will see. A grand bazaar is being held there, or an Exhibition as everyone is calling it. It has been mounted by the WSPU to raise money for the cause."

I cannot wait! I shall be surrounded by real suffragettes. All those women I have been reading about for so long. Flora tells me that they have been advertising it in the streets with their very own band.

21st May 1909

I have a desperate urge to contact my mother. I promised never to return, but only because she practically forced me to give my word. Would she hold it against me if I broke that promise now, after four years? Does she miss me? Does she ever think of me? Is she still alive? I would so like to share with her all that is happening to me, to introduce her to my new life.

23rd May 1909

It is settled. Tomorrow, we will visit the Exhibition. That's the exciting news. But after that, in two days' time, I must return to school. The prospect makes me very downhearted. I am having such a wonderful time. The country means nothing to me without Lady Violet there to encourage and befriend me. Here, with Flora, I feel as though I have found a real sister.

Later

A lady called Katherine Mansfield came by this afternoon to lend Flora a volume of John Ruskin's work, *The Stones of Venice*, because Flora is planning a trip to Italy later this summer. Miss Mansfield was invited to stay to tea. I rather liked her. She is originally from New Zealand.

"Do you know the writings of Ruskin?" she asked me. I confessed that I did not.

"Ah, he is one of the greatest writers of English prose. You must read him, particularly if you have ambitions to be a journalist, Dollie. His earlier works on travel and art are quite exceptional."

Then the discussion turned to a Debussy concert she had attended yesterday evening at the Queen's Hall. This was followed by passionate complaints about the stench and pollution caused by motor cars. "There are so many of the blasted things now. Everywhere in this city, the streets reek of petroleum," she cried. "It is not at all like my home town of Wellington. I positively refuse to use one. If I take a cab, it must be a hansom."

Flora hooted with laughter. "Oh, Katherine, my dear, I fear that you will never visit me again!" And she confessed that she has ordered a Fiat motor car, which will be arriving any day now.

Miss Mansfield then told us that in Australia and New Zealand women are far better regarded than in England. In those two far-off antipodean countries, women have already won the vote!

"Melbourne, the last state on the Australian continent to concede it, gave women the vote last year.

Here in England we females are disgracefully discriminated against and oppressed by men," she lamented, and continued by saying that until we have the vote and a voice of our own, nothing will change.

How I agree with her sentiments!

24th May 1909

The Exhibition! Oh, the Exhibition! What sights I have seen and what a secret adventure I have made of it.

First, we visited two replica prison cells. I went inside one of them and walked around. It was eerie! And so cramped. They had been constructed to demonstrate what women are suffering on our behalf, the conditions they are being forced to endure for the sake of what they believe is our right. And it *is* our right. Women should have a voice in this country. In every country.

Afterwards, to brighten our mood, we ate the most delicious ice cream from a stall set up by Americans, and then we paraded up and down the alleys, in amongst the busy throng of chattering people, peering at all the goods on offer. Of course I had no money to buy anything, but I didn't care. I was there to look, gaze and breathe it all in. We visited stalls with displays of exotic pieces of jewellery, and all sorts of handicrafts. I have never seen so many lace pillowslips and tablecloths! There were kindly stallholders selling books, flowers, herbs, needlework, chinaware, fancy hats and Lord knows what else. There were bands playing rousing music, tables laid out for tea. We made a stop at a booth for the Actresses' Franchise League. Flora, of course, knew everyone and was greeted with much embracing. She introduced me to a group of her actress friends. I do not remember all their names, but Elizabeth Robins, the American woman with the amber beads who was at Flora's the other day, was one of them. Several others were fluttering around a tall, skinny gentleman with a beard. He was wearing a tweed suit and seemed to be holding court, talking rapidly in a thick Irish accent.

"Who's he?" I whispered to Flora.

"His name is George Bernard Shaw, a rather well-known music critic and playwright, and an active supporter of women's rights. He wrote a play two or three years ago, *The Doctor's Dilemma*, whose leading character is named Sir Bloomfield Bonnington. He swears he didn't steal the name from Father," she grinned.

Then, while Flora chatted animatedly to her colleagues, I stood gazing in every direction. There was such a buzz of energy fed by the excitement and the determination to win this battle against the current Liberal government. Well, against all anti-suffrage governments. In fact, against anyone who claims that women are lesser citizens than men and are not capable of understanding politics. Suddenly, my eyes lighted on a stand where a large white, purple and green banner had been hung.

"Do you know what those colours represent?" Elizabeth asked me.

"They are the colours of the Women's Social and Political Union."

"Yes, but why those three in particular?"

I shook my head.

"Purple stands for dignity, white for purity and green for hope. But why don't you go and find out for yourself? Don't worry, I'll tell Flora where you've gone."

"Thank you," I said, hurrying off through the crowds. There were quite a few people queuing to ask questions but eventually I was able to push my way forward to a desk where a red-haired woman with pince-nez was presiding over piles of pamphlets. Her job was to explain to all those interested what the aims of the WSPU are. I told her that I knew all about the fight and that my dream was to become a member.

"Well, why not join now?" she replied in a broad Scottish accent.

"Might I?" I was thrilled at the prospect but also a bit scared. I can't quite explain why. Well, yes, I can. I think it was because I felt as though I was being treacherous to Flora, who had made it clear that she is a suffragist not a suffragette, and that Lady Violet had also leaned towards the less militant approach. Then I reasoned that Lady Violet would want me to be true to myself. Above all else, I believe that is what she would demand of me.

But will it make that much difference if I join? I was asking myself. And my silent response was that these are the women I admire and want to be affiliated with. These are the women, if any, who could change the hardships that housewives such as my mother are forced to endure.

The Scottish lady handed me a form, which I filled in and signed after barely a glance before thrusting it nervously back at her.

She read my name and said, "Welcome, Dollie Baxter. We are delighted that you are with us. Feel free to visit our offices at 4, Clements Inn, whenever you fancy. Think of it as your home. My name is Harriet Kerr and I am the office manager."

"I'll be there, Miss Kerr," I said, and I hurried away in search of Flora.

On our way home in her new Fiat motor car Flora told me more about her Irish playwright friend, Mr Shaw. He's a Socialist and a fighter for the rights of the poor. I am not madly interested in plays – actually, I have never been to a theatre show – but I would dearly love to meet him and ask him many questions.

25th May 1909

Flora is my very best friend and I love her like a sister, but I have not yet plucked up the courage to confess to her that yesterday I joined the suffragettes. Though I did feel desperate enough over breakfast to blurt out my desire not to return to Cheltenham.

"But it is a very fine institute and your education is of the utmost importance, Dollie. Surely you realize that? And Grandma went to such lengths—"

"Yes, I know, but without her close at hand, it will never be the same again. If it's possible, I would prefer to continue my education here. I feel at home in London. Oh, Flora, I would so like my future to be here."

"Well, there is Croydon Girls' High School or Blackheath, but they are long distances out of town. I will make some enquiries. There are sure to be several excellent girls' schools in the city centre, though it may mean that you will need a tutor until we find the right one for you. Leave it with me."

"Thank you. I will be closer to my roots and relatives. Well, to my mother..."

"Is it your wish to return to your birthplace and live with her?"

I remained silent. How many times recently have I asked myself this question? Of course, I know that I cannot stay on indefinitely with Flora... But how can I go back? I know so little of my mother's way of life now; I have become estranged from my past. The fact is, I belong nowhere.

"I don't think so," I answered eventually, "though I long to see her again, to have news of her."

"Have you visited her while you've been in town?"

"Not yet."

"Then why don't we go together? Tomorrow morning, directly after breakfast, we'll take the Fiat and…"

I hesitated, remembering my vow. Flora mistook my hesitation for an unwillingness to include her.

"How thoughtless of me! No, you must go alone. I won't intrude on your life. I only want to assist you as my grandmother has done. When you are ready, let me know what you have decided and I will do everything I can to help you. In the meantime, you are welcome to stay here for as long as you please."

I nodded and smiled at the touch of her hand on mine.

Flora is splendid, but we are so different. Her world is exciting and international, but it is not my way forward. I must make my home where my heart is, where I feel my commitments lie. But first I must learn whatever news there might be of my mother.

26th May 1909

I don't know where to begin to express what I am feeling tonight and all that I have witnessed during the course of this day.

After breakfast, I walked to the southern end of Holborn and from there found a bus that was heading east out of the city centre. I chose a seat by the window so that I could peer out at all the London streetcars and the thoroughfares and the people bustling by. Many of the main roads have been furnished with electric lights now, but there are gas lamps down the narrower side-streets. I needed distraction. I was making my way to the district of my old home in search of my mother and my heart was beating fast with the anticipation of what lay ahead.

The change as we approached the poorer regions of London was obvious to anyone with half an eye. The buildings grew uglier. Even the sky seemed darker as blocks of flats, cheaply constructed and over-populated, closed out the light. The pavements were a sea of concerned faces. We drove by an open market, where children and grown-ups alike were rooting hungrily through garbage piles, salvaging vegetables and fruits and stuffing them directly into their mouths.

Once I stepped off the bus, I meandered for a while up and down the cobbled lanes, lost in the stream of shabby people. I was scared of going to my address, scared of what I would or would not find there. I could not say if, during that walk, I more greatly desired to find my mother or not.

I remember my earlier life as a time of endless hardships. I have grown used to another standard of living and it has softened me. But the trick these past four years has played on my memory was a greater deception than I had bargained for. Today I came face to face with much that I had wiped out. I had forgotten the day-to-day struggles of the thousands living and starving in such nook-and-cranny quarters. Crowds everywhere. Sad, pinched faces with desperate or drunken eyes. All of them facing destitution. You cannot get away from folk in this part of London town. A heaving mass of humanity struggling to make it through one day to the next.

I could not help but see the streets, the lodgings, the second-hand clothes shops, the people sleeping rough without so much as a blanket to keep them warm and dry – the world of East End London in all its sordid detail – through Flora's eyes, not my own, and I felt shame. Not for my kin, but for the fact that the entire locality is shockingly down-at-heel and smells so foul you want to hold your breath. Squalid is the adjective that sprang to mind.

I passed a man swaying on his haunches, trying to mend his shoes. Shoes that weren't fit for the dustbin.

A small grocery store, one of the few I spotted, had signs in the window stating the various prices of the goods on sale. I paused to look. Tea – 1d, Sugar – 1d, Bread – 3d and Butter – 2d.

Usually it had been me who was sent out to buy a small something or other, because I was less likely to be refused the paltry morsels needed to keep our hunger at bay until Father received his next inadequate pay packet.

"Give us tuppence worth of this or thruppence worth of the other," I'd beg the storekeeper. "Mum says she'll square it with you Friday when Dad brings home his wages."

I remembered how two ounces of boiled ham for "tea", our evening meal, was a sumptuous banquet, shared out between the seven of us. A penny tin of condensed milk was also a huge treat.

I walked on, passing by a narrow lane known as Milk Lane. Washing was hanging out to dry in the alleyways. There was not a flower or a plant in sight. The brick houses are built alongside one another, packed tightly together. Unkempt children were playing in the passageways. These infants are not scruffy urchins because of neglect but because no one has enough resources or time to take better care of them. They stared hard and mistrustfully at my passing silhouette or chased after me gazing in awe, holding out their filthy palms, eyes peering out of underfed faces, in the hope of a coin.

It was my clothes that gave me away as a "foreigner". An outsider from the West End. There might as well be a wall between the two London towns.

I passed a young woman with flushed cheeks whose hair was going grey even though she could not have been more than 30; she was stitching the seat of her son's breeches right there in the street. I bent to tighten my bootlaces, an excuse to observe her and to ask myself: Was that how my mother had looked to the Bonnington family that midsummer day in 1900 when she went knocking on their door? She would also have been about 30 at that time.

Finally I turned a corner and came face to face with our cottage. How small it seemed to me today! The door was ajar. I hung back and took a deep breath. My hands were clammy as I lifted my fist to rap on the wood.

"Who'zere?" was the response called from within. It was followed by an awful bout of coughing. Without a word I pushed the door and stepped inside, for I had recognized the voice of my mother.

Her face was pastry-pale, lined and aged almost beyond recognition. Before me stood a stooped old lady. She gazed at me in blank amazement.

"Christ Almighty! Dollie? No, it can't be you."

I noticed bottles of stout, both full and empty, littering the floor. How can she afford such indulgences? I was smiling nervously to encourage the situation. Is she spending whatever food money comes her way on stout? She was painfully thin.

"Yes, it is." I heard the quaver in my speech.

She scrutinized me hard. "Well, take a bloomin' look at yerself. All dressed up."

"I hope you don't mind... I know I promised not to return, but..."

"Quite the lady you've become, eh?"

I looked about me, lost for words. Her scullery-cum-parlour room – there is only the one living space

59

– was hideously cramped and it smelt of old mushrooms. I felt a rush of shame. Not for what I was witnessing but for the privileged existence I have been living. The private rooms with private toilet facilities that I have begun to take for granted. How could I have forgotten so many details, and so quickly? The primitive and inadequate lavatory accommodation out back alongside the coalhole. Cockroaches running haywire up and down the walls.

Mother's room contains a sink, dingy-brown from years of use, which serves for both cooking purposes and washing facilities. Along one wall is a broken-down dresser. On the table stands the same big, enamelled teapot we used when I was a small child.

"I know I promised not to return—"

"So what are you doing here and what the bleedin' 'ell are yer staring at?" she snapped, without the slightest glimmer of warmth.

I wanted to burst into tears. My desire was to run away, to be shot of this scene as soon as possible, but then I reminded myself: *This is your mother*.

I took a deep breath and the reeking odour all but burned my nostrils. "Lady Campbell has passed away," I said.

"Well, there's nothing for you 'ere. I can't keep you. I can't keep meself. It's your brother John what's lookin' after me. I gave you yer chance. If you've made a hash of it…" And as her fury rose, so her breathing grew more irregular and she doubled up with another fit of coughing. I forced her to sit, to be still and silent for a moment. She raised a hand to her mouth. I took a step towards her but her gesture was brusque, warning me to keep my distance.

"I have not come here to be a burden to you," I began firmly. "I only wanted you to know that I shan't be returning to Gloucestershire. I intend to continue my education in London. I intend to find lodgings close by and I thought that…" My sentence dried like wood chips in my mouth. Her hand was still clamped against her lips as she struggled for breath. "Lady Campbell has left me some money. I am not entitled to touch it until I reach 21, but… I want help you. To find you somewhere else to live, to take you away from…"

Her eyes rose to meet my gaze as her hands fell into her lap. I saw then how sick she was. Small and vulnerable like a bird caught in a trap, dying.

"The best thing you can do for me, Dollie, is to make your own way. Don't, for the Lord's sake, get yerself sucked back into any of this."

"What about my brothers? Do they visit and care for you? What are you living on?" I persisted, but she waved her hand in a dismissive way.

"I don't want to see yer here ever again," she rasped, and rose unsteadily to shove me off back into the street. Of course, she had no strength but I went anyway. Perversely, I did it to please her.

But what must I do? How can I help her?

27th May 1909

I woke feeling a heavy responsibility hanging over me. Forcing myself to be decisive, I bathed and dressed quickly. I was intending to discuss my mother's situation with Flora and ask her advice but she had left early for rehearsals of a new film she is involved in, so I skipped breakfast and set off for Clements Inn, to the offices of the WSPU, my thoughts still troubled by my visit of yesterday.

"The abyss" is the phrase coined by certain writers and journalists to describe the conditions of the life of the poor in this country. "The people of the abyss" wrote the best-selling author, HG Wells, when speaking of Britain's working class. And how right he is!

I know for sure that *when* women are given the vote the living conditions of the poor will be one of the first problems to be addressed. And that is why I decided to call at the WSPU today. If there is one thing that I can do for my mother it is to fight for women and our place in this society. And, once that fight has been won, then we will be well placed to look to our society. A society that is sinking at its foundations.

I reached Clements Inn, opened the door and found myself in a large, immaculately tidy room, where girls at typewriters were clacking busily. There were posters on all the walls, stacks of newspapers on the floor, neat piles of banners, legal books and social texts everywhere.

I enquired for Harriet Kerr, who welcomed me as though I were a friend and then introduced me to a middle-aged woman, Miss Baker. Astoundingly, I learned that she had been Flora's governess for many years. Now she is employed as a member of the staff for the movement, or "the Cause" as they all call it there.

"How old are you, Dollie?" asked Miss Baker.

"I have just turned fifteen," I fibbed. In fact, I shall be fifteen in November.

"Why aren't you at school?"

I considered her question. The quarter of London where I originally came from has no library. Why would it have? Most women in such districts are illiterate. A few of the men can read a newspaper and write their names, even a letter if they are obliged to, but what time do they have for reading? Children leave school at eight or nine and go out to work because the families desperately need the pittance of income their offspring earn. My brothers were all working by the age of ten. I would have been engaged in domestic work if Fate had not taken a hand. I wanted to tell all this to Miss Baker, but I liked her and decided not to be cheeky. "I have recently moved back to London and hope to start at a new school in the autumn."

Miss Baker screwed up her brow. "You should be attending school."

"I believe Flora is looking for a temporary tutor for me," I answered.

"I see. Well, while you have time to spare, just say the word and we'll take you on as a volunteer."

"What would it involve?"

"Can you type?"

I shook my head.

"Never mind, there are plenty of other duties to be carried out. But only in your free time. One of our goals is to encourage women's education, not to hinder it, do you understand me?"

I nodded.

"How about selling copies of our suffrage newspaper, *Votes for Women*? It means going out on the streets. Or if you are too timid for that we could put you to enrolling new members. Or interviewing local MPs."

"I can't afford to get into any trouble…"

Miss Baker laughed loudly. "Not all of the ladies here are of a militant mind, Dollie. Harriet, who enrolled you at the Exhibition, left her secretarial agency in Aberdeen to come and work here, but she has made it a condition of her employment that her work is exclusively administrative."

"I would be honoured to help out in whatever way I can," I replied.

"Excellent! Why don't we start with something straightforward such as the door-to-door distribution of handbills, or…"

"My dream is to become a journalist, so why don't I try my hand at selling the newspapers?"

"Splendid! Now what are you doing for the rest of the day?"

I shrugged.

"Then why don't we begin immediately? This was going to be a free day for me and I was on my way to a new Monet exhibition at the National Gallery, but that can wait. I'll go later. Are you familiar with the work of the French Impressionists?"

I shook my head.

"Even better. I will accompany you on your newspaper expedition. Just this once, mind, so that you get the hang of it, and while we are out and about I can answer any questions you might have about the Cause. Then later this afternoon, we'll make an outing together to the National Gallery." And, with that, Miss Baker flung a huge batch of papers at me, shoved a hat carelessly on her head, wrapped a light shawl round her shoulders and we stepped out into the street.

We made our way by underground to the corner of Tottenham Court Road and Oxford Street. "This will be your pitch. Be warned, it's a busy one. You'll sell a good stack of papers here and you will almost certainly get asked questions about our work. So you'd better have your facts straight. No, don't stand there. It is important to position yourself in the gutter. Never stand on the pavements."

"Why ever not?" I asked, fearing the passage of hansoms and, worse, of motor cars.

"Because you run the risk of being charged by the police with obstruction."

"Oh." This news made me a little panicky. In my heart I want to be a true and brave suffragette, but in reality, I cannot afford to get myself into trouble.

"Don't be anxious. There's nothing to worry about. Here comes someone. Offer the paper."

And before I knew what was happening I was selling my first copy to a smiling, elderly lady who donated not the requested one penny price but a full shilling and then complimented me on the splendid work we are doing!

Later, over a mug of tea near Oxford Circus, I was introduced to another newish recruit, Mary Richardson, a Canadian, who has been in England since 1900. Mary is selling papers a little way up the street from my pitch.

"The main thing is not to be shy and not to take any abuse hurled at you personally," she advised me.

"What sort of abuse?"

"Now, don't go scaring our Dollie away," laughed Miss Baker. "Mary was bombarded with rotten fruit by some women working in the Crosse & Blackwell factory."

"Whatever for?" I was beginning to doubt my commitment to the Cause!

"There are many women and men too, who continue to believe that our sole purpose on this earth is to breed and be perfect wives. They see our work as a threat. Or they have the notion that we are demeaning ourselves, giving females a bad name. 'Respectable women stay home,' they say. 'It is only the other kind of woman who makes a spectacle of herself in the street.'

"Others declare that our force is made up of spinsters and widows, that we are women lacking men. All nonsense, of course, and makes me quite furious, but we must be patient. Sooner or later they will come to see that our place is right alongside men, making decisions, weighing up the choices, taking responsibility for the way the world works. I personally believe that when that day comes, folk will see that there are certain areas in the public arena that will be better handled by women."

"Such as?" I asked.

"Well, we are not warmongers, for a start. We don't run round with weapons. I think the chances of international peace would be increased if the government had women in the cabinet negotiating on their behalf. Who knows, we might have avoided the Boer War."

Gosh, I had never considered such a notion before, but it made sense.

Miss Baker then recounted to us the episode of last year when she and several other WSPU colleagues went to Downing Street where one of their suffrage sisters was intending to speak. Miss Nell chained herself to the railings outside the Prime Minister's front door so that the police could not move her along before she had finished her speech. She was keen that the Cabinet, who were in session, as well as the crowd gathering in the street, would hear her words without interruption. "And what an impassioned address it was!" grinned Miss Baker.

"What did she say?" I asked.

"'Each and every female in this country of eighteen years and older should have the right to vote in this nation's political elections. We have the right to be equal with men. We *are* the equal of men. It is they who are denying us our rights and our true position in the society that we are also building. This battle is about more than the vote. It is about equal opportunities!' She was quite remarkable. A blazing force wrapped in chains, a human letter from us all. Flora was with us in the crowd on that occasion. I wish she'd come along more often. Soon another woman, a nurse, Olivia Smith, rushed forward and followed Miss Nell's example. Imagine it, Dollie, two women chained to the railings in Downing Street. The police could do nothing. The crowd grew excited. Some were angry and jeered as the women spoke out. Others were cheering them on. It was a thrilling and a dangerous moment. I rushed forward, intent on joining my sisters, but Harriet held me back." Miss Baker paused and took a sip of her tea.

"Why did she do that?"

"I explained to you earlier, Harriet is not militant and she believes that there is important work to be done behind the scenes, in the offices. I am needed for that work because as a trained teacher I can write the pamphlet literature, and correct the spelling and details."

"What happened to the two women?" I asked.

"They were arrested. And two others with them. The police hauled all four off to Bow Street

Magistrates' Court, where they were charged with disorderly conduct, found guilty and sentenced to three weeks' imprisonment or to pay hefty fines. All chose prison because it creates publicity for our cause. Good Lord, look at the time! We must dash, Dollie, if we are to make the gallery. Now then, Mary, you take Dollie's remaining newspapers and sell them for us, will you, dear? Thank you. We'll see you tomorrow."

And with that we were gone and off to the Monet exhibition. It was quite wonderful. Such colours, soft as butterfly wings. But I will have to write about that adventure tomorrow because now I am exhausted. My feet are killing me and Flora has guests for dinner. I intend to wear one of my new frocks.

28th May 1909

I spent about half an hour yesterday standing in front of a painting entitled *Waterlilies*, painted by Claude Monet in 1903. I don't think that I have ever seen anything so lovely. It is curious because when you move up close you can see clearly that the canvas is a mass of painted dots. The idea is that, joined together, they give the impression of a shape or a colour or a scene. That is why he and other artists painting in the same style are known as "Impressionists". According to Miss Baker there is an entire school of painters in France who have been christened "French Impressionists". Not "school" as in my one at Cheltenham, but as in "school of thought": a way of thinking. The Impressionists have a way of looking at light and its effect on objects and nature. Wandering through the exhibition, gazing at all those canvases, it was as though someone had drawn back the curtains on to a new world, a new mode of *seeing*. I have never perceived life, looked at nature, from such a perspective before. It was so beautiful. It really lifted my mood.

I so like Miss Baker. It would be too wonderful if she could be my summer tutor. I shall suggest it to Flora.

29th May 1909

Trying to find time to spend with Flora is so difficult. She has been busy working on a film and there have been so many visitors. Luckily, this evening I found her alone in her room. She was curled up in a flowery kimono, on her chaise longue, hair flowing long and loose, barefoot, reading a script, with the two Russian Blue cats, Strindberg and Ibsen, dozing at her side.

I wasted no time in asking if I could possibly withdraw a portion of the money that Lady Violet put in trust for me.

Flora looked astonished. "It is not within my power to authorize that," she said. "Is there something you need?"

I explained that I had been to see my mother. "I fear she may be seriously ill and needs urgent medical care. I must have money to help her."

Flora tossed her script to the carpeted floor. "But, Dollie, it is locked away. The terms of the will have to be respected; that is the law. But I can come with you to meet your mother. I could bring a doctor who can examine her. Then we'll know what needs to be done. And you are not to concern yourself with the costs."

I stroked one of the cats, thinking about what Flora had offered. "I don't know that my mother would be willing to see a doctor."

"A close friend of mine, Caroline Sturge, is a doctor. She's very kind. Why don't we give her a try?"

I agreed that we should, and once I had made the decision I felt as though a great load had been lifted from me.

"That's settled then. Now, please be a sweetheart and take me through my lines."

30th May 1909

I entered the cottage first, intending to prepare Mother for the arrival of the others, and was utterly shocked by what I saw. I could not believe that she had deteriorated so quickly, nor that she had been left alone in such a condition.

"Who's been looking after you?" I cried. "Where's John?"

"What're yer doing bringing those bleedin' toffs here?" she hissed as Flora and Doctor Sturge entered. "Who are they?"

I did not dare to give Flora's family name. I asked after my brother again, but Mother could barely talk. I think her initial outburst had weakened her. I glanced about but saw no signs of a male presence. At least he must be feeding and keeping her or she would have found herself on the streets, in pauper lodgings or the workhouse long ago.

Judging by the grave expression on Doctor Sturge's face, she seemed to recognize the nature of Mother's sickness even before she had examined her.

"She needs immediate medical care," she said.

"Is she going to die?" I croaked.

"Not if we get her to a hospital right now."

It was a real battle to move her. She may have been weak and very ill but she put up an almighty resistance. "The only way you'll get me out of 'ere is in a bandbox," she rasped.

"What's a bandbox?" whispered Flora.

"A coffin."

Eventually she agreed to go. As they carried her out

75

on the stretcher, I saw the dark vermilion stains on her fingers and realized she must have been coughing up blood. Thank Heaven we got here in time.

31st May 1909

My mother has been taken to St Thomas's Hospital. Whitechapel would have been closer but both Flora and the doctor agreed that it is desperately overcrowded and both staff and facilities are inadequate.

I visited her there today. Dr Sturge and another doctor were examining her and I was only allowed to stay for a minute. She seemed pleased to see me though, and I promised to return again soon.

2nd June 1909

Dr Sturge telephoned Flora late this afternoon. She confirmed that my mother's lymph glands are very enlarged and that she is suffering from a form of tuberculosis.

"Promise me she won't die," I cried when I heard the diagnosis.

"We are doing everything we can," she answered.

I felt totally depressed when I put down the phone and spent the evening alone in my room.

6th June 1909

Flora and I have been to visit two schools. The headmistresses interviewed us, asked me questions about my time in Cheltenham and requested a report from my former school. One is in Hammersmith in the west of London and the other is in Camden, a little north of Flora's house. St Paul's, the one in Hammersmith, also made me sit a short written exam. The paper was not difficult, but my heart was not in it. I cannot stop worrying about my mother. Both schools said they would be writing to us shortly.

11th June 1909

No new school has been settled yet, so Flora was delighted at the suggestion that Miss Baker should tutor me in the meantime.

"But how did you come to meet her, Dollie?"

I could not lie. I owned up to the fact that it was a contact made on the day we visited the Exhibition.

"I see. Well, she is a brilliant woman and a first-class teacher. I only hope that she does not allow her allegiance to the WSPU to colour your studies. I will need her assurance on that point."

12th June 1909

Miss Baker came to have tea with us. Flora and she were obviously delighted to see one another again and they have settled on an arrangement. Five sessions a week is what they have scheduled, so that I don't fall behind with my lessons. We will study in the living room between eight and ten each morning. The hours are a bit early for my liking but Miss Baker needs to be at the WSPU offices by half-past ten.

13th June 1909

Lessons began today with a series of oral tests: maths followed by French. Then Miss Baker quizzed me on geography, a bit of English literature and history and, to round it all off, German verbs.

"Mmm," she pronounced. "Your maths and German are extremely weak. Your geography is reasonable, your history is rusty and English literature quite good. We have a lot to do."

Once all that was over, she set me pages of questions to prepare for tomorrow's session.

When Flora asked me later how the session had gone, I told her, "Miss Baker is horribly keen on German."

She laughed and said that she remembered that.

14th June 1909

I went to the WSPU today and helped to prepare pamphlets for distribution. Miss Baker and I sat cross-legged on the floor, slipping them into envelopes while she took me through some Latin grammar. I have forgotten everything! After we had completed several boxloads we stopped for a cup of tea and she and Harriet astounded me with episodes of their suffrage experiences.

I learned that on 11th October last year, Emmeline and Christabel Pankhurst, together with another suffragette, Flora Drummond, addressed huge crowds from the plinth of Nelson's Column in Trafalgar Square. Thousands of handbills were distributed. They were printed with the message: *Men and Women, help the Suffragettes to Rush the House of Commons on Tuesday Evening, 13th October 1908 at 7.30 pm.*

Miss Baker remembered that it had been a warm day, the end of a long hot summer, and all the while she was distributing her leaflets she had been aware of the eyes of the police upon her. They were stationed everywhere.

"The bobbies were keeping track of us, Dollie. By then we were beginning to realize that they had been ordered to spy on our every meeting, to keep abreast of what we were up to. Two days later, on 13th October, the WSPU held their demonstration as planned, but the bobbies were waiting and there were violent clashes. The police had instructions to keep the women out of the House. Twenty-four women were arrested, including Emmeline Pankhurst, who was sentenced to three months in prison. Over the remaining months of 1908 suffragettes continued to attempt to gatecrash Parliament. The police, both on foot and on horseback, began to respond with violence. Women were hurt. Many were arrested and imprisoned.

"Until last year, 'Deeds not Words' had become a passionate call but had remained a non-violent interpretation of what was needed to bring about change. Now we feel we must go further," said Miss Baker, "in order that the Cause be brought to everyone's attention. We are frustrated by the deaf ears of our Parliament but we remain resolved. Our government will hear what we have to say even if we must break the law to make them listen."

Harriet went on to explain that some Union members have been disguising themselves as waitresses and messenger boys, jumping out of delivery vans, hanging from the windows of the House of Commons, entering from the River Thames, haranguing MPs wherever and whenever they can. Nothing will stop them, not even the prospect of months behind bars.

"But if the law forces us to serve sentences, what we are insisting upon is to be classed as First Division prisoners. That is to say, political prisoners rather than common criminals."

"I don't understand the difference," I replied.

"Well," said Miss Baker, "First Division status gives us certain rights or privileges that are denied to Second or Third Division offenders. For example,

First Division prisoners are not searched when admitted to jail. They can order in food if they wish to, and most do because prison food is terrible. They are allowed visitors, books, newspapers and writing materials, and they are allowed to pen articles for publication. Also they are free to spend time with fellow inmates. Last year, when Christabel and Emmeline were in Holloway, they were separated. Emmeline was tagged a 'dangerous criminal' and kept in solitary confinement. This meant no exercise, no chapel, no companionship, for days at a time during her sentence."

"That's horrible." I was beginning to understand the sacrifices involved in being a true suffragette. If I was faced with such horrors I am not sure that I would have the courage to stand them.

15th June 1909

At the hospital this afternoon one of the nurses warned me that Mother's condition is rather advanced, but she assured me that she is comfortable and they are doing everything they can.

I sat with her for a little while but she was weak and her eyes were closed most of the time – she was dozing, I think – so I just held her hand and kept quiet.

23rd June 1909

I sat in on a thrillingly heated debate at the WSPU offices yesterday. The subject was: How to guarantee that any sentenced suffragette will serve her term as a First Division prisoner.

"I intend to write a letter to Parliament demanding that our status as political prisoners be recognized," announced Miss Baker. This was received by applause.

"Throughout the civilized world, male political offenders are given special status and we have the right to receive the same treatment as men," a woman whom I had not seen before called out.

"Yes!" a chorus of voices rejoined, including mine.

Someone suggested, and it was backed up by Mary Richardson standing near me, that the younger, stronger women should volunteer to serve the prison sentences, which are debilitating for the older women.

"That's a good point," Harriet Kerr said. "We all know that Emmeline's health is not what it was."

I knew I should volunteer, but after all that Miss Baker had told me I felt too scared. Solitary confinement would terrify me. A few put their hands up and called out their names. I did not, and then the moment was lost because a Scottish woman whose name is Marion – she's a painter or sculptress, I think – hurried to the front of the room, signalled for quiet and began to speak.

"Ladies, I think there are two issues that need to be considered here. The first is that the government's treatment of suffrage campaigners is barbaric. Of course, we are not thieves or murderesses. There is no question that any status given to us other than that of political prisoners is a deliberate misinterpretation of the law. We are fighting for our rights, and that is not a crime." There was cheering and waving from the entire room, but Marion raised her hand for hush. "Wait, wait. Because this is about much more than what status we are given as prisoners. The fact is we shouldn't be thrown into gaol at all. *We are legally entitled to petition.*" Marion's speech was wildly applauded and the evening ended on a very upbeat note.

Walking to the bus I was still asking myself whether or not I should volunteer. So far I have done little for the Cause besides sell newspapers. But if I did have to go to prison, what about my school work? Or even worse, what if something were to happen to my mother and I wasn't there?

24th June 1909

Marion Wallace Dunlop, the Scottish painter who spoke at the debate yesterday evening, rubber-stamped a message across one of the walls at St Stephen's Hall in the House of Commons this morning. The extract is from the 1689 Bill of Rights:

It is the right of the subjects to petition the King, and all commitments and prosecutions for such petitioning are illegal.

Of course, she has been arrested. But what is excellent is that she is stating a very important point. What is more, she is not alone in claiming that we have every right to protest and that we cannot be arrested or imprisoned for the simple act of petitioning.

25th June 1909

Flora told me this morning that she is leaving for Italy at the beginning of July. She is intending to visit Florence and Venice, and expects to be away for a couple of months. She invited me to accompany her but I declined, which surprised her.

I want to be close to my mother, I told her. Also, I feel there is too much happening here to go off travelling. This is a very important time for the Cause and I want to involve myself more deeply. Marion Wallace Dunlop's claim that it is our right as citizens to be allowed to protest is being taken up as a legal battle among the suffragettes. If the Cause wins this point, none of us can ever again be imprisoned for demonstrating for our rights.

I would certainly feel less guilty then about the fact that I have not volunteered for anything more dangerous than office work or newspaper-selling. And I thought I was brave!

30th June 1909

Marion has been sentenced to serve a month in Holloway Prison on a charge of wilful damage. She has been classed as a Second Division prisoner but is fighting against such treatment and insisting that she be moved to the First Division. The request has been refused by Mr Herbert Gladstone, the Home Secretary.

A letter from the school in north London arrived today. Flora said that they have not accepted me. No reason was given.

"Don't be disappointed. There's still St Paul's," she said. "If not, we'll try others. And Miss Baker will continue to tutor you until you are settled."

Lord, I feel a real failure.

5th July 1909

Something quite extraordinary and unforeseen has happened. Marion Wallace Dunlop has thrown away the food that has been brought to her and decided on a hunger strike. This is her own idea. No one at the WSPU knew a thing about it. Several members spoke of the dangers to her health when the news reached us, but most of us saw it as an act of real courage and daring.

The prison authorities are threatening to force-feed her through her nostrils with a liquid mixture of egg and milk. Ugh, how disgusting!

6th July 1909

Miss Baker told me that the wardresses have been leaving trays of food in Marion's cell in the hope that she will weaken and break her fast. So far she has stood firm. We are all keeping our fingers crossed that Mr Asquith will relent and improve her prison status.

Flora set off on her travels this morning. I was really sad to see her go. I hugged her tightly and thanked her for allowing me to remain on here, and for all her many kindnesses to me and to my mother, who has grown a little stronger these last few days. When I visited her this afternoon she was quite chirpy and talked about going home soon. I pray it won't be too long before she is allowed to leave the hospital, but I hate the idea of her returning to the East End.

When I arrived back at the house, it felt so empty. I wandered about from room to room, not knowing what to do with myself. Then I sat on the sofa with the two cats at my side and read *A Midsummer Night's Dream* – Miss Baker is going to set me an exam on Shakespeare.

I have promised myself to use these weeks fruitfully, to work hard at my studies and prepare myself well for whichever new school takes me.

9th July 1909

Marion has been released! After 91 hours of fasting, almost four days, the Home Secretary has set her free.

Emmeline Pankhurst, who is away, travelling from one corner of Britain to the next, talking to groups, at societies, and raising the profile of the Cause, has stated that this act of Marion's has lifted "our militant movement on to a higher and more heroic plane".

I am so proud to be a member of the Union.

When I popped into the hospital to see Mother I was dying to tell her some of the WSPU news and all that is happening to me, but two of my brothers were there with their wives and children and Mother looked tired and weak again. So I only stayed a while and came home.

I feel very distanced from my family and I suspect my brothers resent me. I know my oldest brother's wife, Clara, does. I can tell by the way she looks at me. And one of my nephews, Henry junior, said to me, "You talk funny."

20 July 1909

Talk at the WSPU offices today was that Marion's example has been followed by other imprisoned suffragettes. Fourteen women who were convicted of stone-throwing on 12th July have taken up her baton. When their request to Mr Gladstone to be transferred to the First Division was turned down, they refused to wear their prison clothes or to clean up their cells. They have broken windows to get fresh air and the prison authorities have responded by throwing them into punishment cells for their disobedience.

"We are political prisoners and you are treating us like common criminals," was the women's response. They have all decided to go on hunger strike.

26th July 1909

The women have been released.

This is being hailed as a triumph for our cause because although the authorities threatened forcible feeding they have not carried out the threat. The general consensus seems to be that they do not dare because it would be barbaric and illegal, and would cause public anger.

I received a letter from Flora this morning. It was sent from Paris. She has been staying for a few days with Alice Guy on her way south. Flora sounded very happy about a scheme she and Alice have for directing a film together. I wonder if this means that she will be away longer than she originally intended. I hope not. I miss her and I want to talk to her about my mother's future.

A letter also arrived from St Paul's in Hammersmith, addressed to Flora. I am *dying* to know what it says.

14th August 1909

After lunch, I took the bus to St Thomas's and went to visit my mother. She was very pale, but although still frail she looked a little plumper. She coughs incessantly, but tries her best to make light of her pains in front of me. I think I am rather bad at hiding my feelings; and she senses how upset I get.

We talked of when she leaves the hospital. I suggested finding her a little flat near to Flora. "We'd share it," I promised, but she flatly refuses to move from that horrid damp cottage. How stubborn she is and how frustrated it makes me. But I must be positive. It is wonderful to see her growing stronger and to know that she is going to get better and that somehow or other we will work the other problems out.

20th August 1909

It is now illegal for women to attend public gatherings, particularly those events organized by or involving the Liberal party. The government is embarrassed by the heckling they are receiving.

As a protest, a group of us, including Mary Richardson and Miss Baker, hid in the bushes last night outside a hall in Kentish Town where a Liberal meeting was assembling. While the hall was filling up we tried to make our way inside, but we were forced back out on to the street. So we remained outside, shouting, "Votes for Women!"

"Why don't you treat imprisoned suffragettes as political prisoners?" I called nervously. My heart was beating fast. I've never heckled before.

Mary followed with, "Put your Liberal principles into practice."

"Justice, and the vote for women!" That was me again. I was beginning to gain confidence.

"Give us the vote and we'll go home," yelled Miss Baker. What a booming voice she has!

People in the hall turned their heads in horror. "Get those blasted women away from here!" A short, bald-headed chap instructed as the doors were closed in our faces. We tried one more time to get in by beating our fists against the doors, but we had no luck. We hung about outside in the street, shouting and kicking up a racket, until eventually, hoarse and hungry, we took a bus back into town and went for soup and ice cream and cake at Mary's. All of us were laughing, buoyed and exhilarated by what we had done. It felt so daring.

21st August 1909

Mr Asquith, the Prime Minister, was interrupted during his speech in Liverpool last night. To protest against the bar on women at public meetings, a few suffragettes broke windows and threw stones. They were arrested.

At the office this afternoon, Mary Richardson said to me, "Next time, we'll break a window or two. It's what we should have done last night, eh?"

I shrugged, but I'm not sure I'd dare go that far.

1st September 1909

Flora is back, looking radiant. It was wonderful to see her.

"How's your mother?" she asked me during dinner.

"They say she'll be coming out of hospital very soon," I replied.

"That's wonderful news, but you don't look very happy about it, Dollie."

"I don't want her to go back to our old home," I said. "She'll only get sick again." But I refused to discuss the subject further. I fear Flora will think that I am angling for more assistance, which I am not.

2nd September 1909

Miss Baker was taking me through her corrections on a Charles Dickens essay she had set when Flora came bursting into the living room waving a letter.

"Forgive me for butting in, but this was among my pile of post. It is from St Paul's. You've been granted a place. Well done! Their new year begins on 10th September, which means that we have a mountain of things to organize."

Gosh, school. I have enjoyed all these free days and was beginning to hope that it would never happen.

10th September 1909

It feels so strange to be back in a classroom. I have grown used to a life in London that does not include uniforms, morning assemblies, chapel and structured timetables and I don't like being back in the system one bit. I would far rather Miss Baker continued to tutor me, but I daren't say so to Flora who has gone to such lengths to get me here. We seem to have done nothing but traipse round the shops buying clothes and sportswear and pens and books.

I am one of two new girls. The others in my class have all been here for several years. I am reminded of my first days at Cheltenham Ladies' College and how out of place I felt. Once again, I appear to be the only girl from a working-class background. Of course, no one knows my history because my address is Flora's and my school records are from Cheltenham, but it still makes me feel awkward.

I really MUST NOT be so negative. I dream of being a journalist and of helping my mother. Without a decent education I will have no chance, so I'd better make the best of it. And once I have made some friends, it will be different.

18th September 1909

I was going through my things last night and came across my suffrage scrapbook. I haven't looked at it since moving to London. It seems sort of quaint to me now that I actually know some of the women involved in the struggle. I shall take it to school and work on it as a modern history project – it will help me feel less distanced from the movement.

Asquith was speaking in Birmingham last night. Some regional WSPU members climbed up on to the roof of a neighbouring building, lifted off some slates and hurled them at his car as it drew up. Windows and lamps were smashed, but they were careful to avoid hitting the Prime Minister himself. Their intention was to be heard, not to cause physical violence. They yelled out to him that we won't give up until we have the vote. The police were called and hosepipes were turned on the women, who were driven down by the force of the water and by stones thrown at them. They were led away to prison, soaked to the skin, having lost their shoes in the struggle. One of them was injured, but the article didn't report the seriousness of the injury.

I almost wish that I had been there. I can't imagine myself smashing windows, throwing slates at cars or being arrested, but anything is better than sitting in a classroom all day. School is *so* lady-like.

21st September 1909

The Birmingham demonstrators have been arrested and have received sentences of three and, in Mary Leigh's case, four months. They are now in Winson Green prison in Birmingham, on hunger strike. The authorities are refusing to release them. Instead they have begun the unthinkable: they are force-feeding our women!

Flora and I talked about the matter over breakfast after she had read out a letter in this morning's *Times* written by Christabel Pankhurst. Christabel has stated that women are being driven to stone-throwing by the government. They are banned from attending public meetings and Mr Asquith continues to refuse to meet with the Union and will not discuss the matter. Every avenue to the vote is being blocked.

"I think these acts will do more harm than good," said Flora.

"But what else can we do?" I retaliated.

"*We*? I sincerely hope, Dollie, that you are not involved with such carryings-on. I told you that I do not approve of unconstitutional acts to win the vote. I am as passionate about our place in society as you are, but these methods will not gain us respect. In fact, I believe they will turn public support against us."

I finished my tea and set off for school without another word. During morning break, I asked one of my classmates, Celia, who seems rather nice, what she thinks about the Birmingham women's fate. Her answer was worse than Flora's.

"They deserve to be force-fed," she said.

I'd better keep my opinions to myself then.

24th September 1909

I attended a meeting at the WSPU offices this evening. It is the first I have been to since school began. Usually I arrive early and make tea. We always serve cakes on these occasions, but as a mark of respect tonight we drank water. The place was packed. Women had come long distances to be with us. Christabel Pankhurst was chairing the evening. There was real concern about the welfare of the imprisoned women.

The meeting began with the reading of a letter written by our treasurer, Mrs Emmeline Pethwick-Lawrence, and published in today's edition of *Votes for Women*. Naturally, it denounces the force-feeding of women. It received applause and cheers. Questions followed. These were answered by Christabel, who assured us that her mother has a plan. She stated that, as leaders of the WSPU, she and her mother and Mrs Pethwick-Lawrence are officially supporting the acts of the prisoners, including the stone-throwing, and that they intend to make a public statement tomorrow.

During the break, the point at which we usually serve tea, I heard one or two members suggesting that Emmeline and Christabel had no choice but to stand behind the stone-throwers, even though the Birmingham women acted on their own initiative. I have no idea whether this is true or not.

Afterwards, another letter was read aloud to us, a truly shocking one. It had been written to Marion Wallace Dunlop by a force-fed prisoner and described her ordeal. When Marion had finished, the room was silent. Another lady, who announced herself as a doctor, rose to inform us that the inserted tubes used for force-feeding are frequently unsterilized and infection is possible.

I walked to the bus with Harriet Kerr, but we didn't talk much. I think we both felt sickened.

25th September 1909

Today Mrs Pankhurst, Christabel and Mrs Pethwick-Lawrence have publicly supported the imprisoned women and denounced the government for inflicting such pain and humiliation on them.

At school, one of the teachers talked about what was happening. It turned into a class debate and I was relieved to discover that many of the girls were strongly against the government's actions.

Celia and I ate our lunch together. She seemed less disapproving of the Birmingham women today – I think the debate this morning has made her reconsider her opinions – and I offered to lend her my suffrage scrapbook. "It might give you an idea how long this battle has been going on," I said.

I sat next to a sweet old lady on the bus this evening who said she "had never heard the like in all her years". Personally, I feel so angry and frustrated that it makes me want to run round the streets of London, breaking windows and shouting.

28th September 1909

When I arrived home from school this evening, Mrs Millicent Fawcett was visiting with Flora. Flora called me into the drawing room to be introduced. I did not mention that Lady Violet had presented me to her ages ago in Gloucestershire.

"I want you to hear this, Dollie," Flora said, and because their expressions were both so serious, I thought I must have done something wrong.

Mrs Fawcett then informed me that she had recently written to the Prime Minister requesting an audience with him.

"Do you know what he has answered, Dollie?" Flora asked me.

I shook my head. The way they both quizzed me I felt personally responsible.

"He has refused to see me," Mrs Fawcett explained flatly. "Do you know why?"

Again, I shook my head.

"His argument is that, although I am not connected with the troublemakers, the organization discrediting the case for women's franchise, he is too busy with urgent political business to see anyone from any group connected to the Women's Suffrage movement."

I glanced at Flora who was staring hard at me.

"Forgive me if this sounds impolite," I said. "I really don't intend it to, but this government has slammed the door on all peaceable negotiations and now it criticizes us because we have been driven to other means!"

"*Us*? Dollie, are you telling me that you are involved in these terrible acts?"

I couldn't speak.

"Dollie, Flora has told me all about you and I think it is splendid that you are so committed to our cause," Mrs Fawcett continued quickly, "but won't you put your energies with us? We will win the vote, but we will do it without acts of violence and without turning the British public against us."

I agreed to think about it and then excused myself, saying that I had homework to do. I hurried to my room, feeling – what? Betrayed by Flora, I think.

29th September 1909

Mr Keir Hardie was one of the guests at dinner this evening. What a nice man he is! Inevitably the conversation turned to the hunger strikes and the government's response.

"I don't know how this Liberal government hopes to regain respect. Force-feeding women is barbaric." The voice of Virginia Stephen. "As an eminent Labour MP, Keir, what is your opinion?"

Mr Hardie then recounted how he had challenged the government in the House yesterday. "I begged to know how a Liberal government could justify an act of such cruelty against the female sex. In answer, I was informed by the Home Secretary's speaker that it is common practice in hospitals to force-feed patients when they refuse to eat."

Elizabeth Robins, also a guest, was furious when she heard this. "What nonsense!" she cried. "The only patients who are force-fed in hospitals are the mentally insane."

"Asquith is refusing to meet with Millicent, saying that if he sees her he must also give an audience to the WSPU, but, whatever his excuses, he will be forced to put an end to this inhumanity. His government is being condemned from every quarter," were Flora's words on the subject.

"Might the Home Secretary, the government and prison authorities judge suffrage women mentally unstable?" I ventured. "Perhaps that's the message they want to put across to the British people?"

"That's a very good question!" bellowed Mr Hardie.

I blushed, but was thrilled to have been taken seriously.

4th October 1909

No school today. So I went to the WSPU.

Miss Baker, who I haven't seen in ages, asked me

about my new school. I told her it was fine but that I preferred being tutored by her.

"Have you made any friends yet?"

"There's a nice girl, Celia Loverton, but she isn't madly interested in our cause and she's posh, so… What's been happening here?" I changed the subject because I am fed up with everyone asking me about school.

"Letters are arriving by the sackload at the offices of all the national newspapers in protest against the treatment of the Birmingham women," Miss Baker said, handing me a copy of the latest issue of *Votes for Women*. "Emmeline has written an article in which she demands: 'How can a Liberal government in free England torture women in an attempt to crush their struggle for citizenship rights?' She intends to begin proceedings against the Home Secretary and the prison authorities on the grounds that a physical assault has been committed against these women. She is choosing one prisoner from the group, Mary Leigh, and will fight it as a test case."

"That's a terrific idea!" I cried. "She's bound to win."

6th October 1909

Asquith has received a protest letter signed by 116 doctors opposing the force-feeding of women prisoners:

We the undersigned, being medical practitioners, do most urgently protest against the treatment of artificial feeding of the Suffragist prisoners now in Birmingham Gaol.

We submit to you, that this method of feeding when the patient resists is attended with the gravest of risks, that unforeseen accidents are liable to occur, and that the subsequent health of the person may be seriously injured. In our opinion this action is unwise and inhumane...

I believe my mother's doctor, Caroline Sturge, is on the list.

Editors are resigning from their newspapers if their journal expresses support for the government on this issue.

It is true to say that this has caused a national outcry, both from suffrage sympathizers and opponents alike. And so it should. But the depressing fact is that the Prime Minister is still adamantly refusing to back a women's suffrage bill. Nothing we do or say seems to make any difference.

10th November 1909

My birthday. Fifteen years old. Flora has given me the most wonderful gift in the world. My very own typewriter! I cannot begin to describe how touched I am by her generosity. It made me ashamed for the anger I have felt towards her lately.

Celia gave me a new scrapbook. I was amazed. She really enjoyed my suffrage one. "I hadn't really understood before what it was all about," she said.

I invited her to come to Clements Inn with me, to one of the monthly meetings. She said that she'd think about it.

I visited Mother this evening. She looked much stronger and was happy to see me. We talked about school, but when I spoke of the WSPU she waved her hand impatiently. "You'll end up in trouble mixing with that lot. I don't want you going against Flora," she warned. "She may be a toff, but you are bloody lucky to have 'er."

Sometimes I feel quite on my own. But I am happy about Celia. I want to introduce her to Miss Baker.

11th December 1909

What a bitterly disappointing end to one of the most pressing issues of this year. Mrs Pankhurst's case against the Home Secretary and the prison authorities, which she has been fighting for the past two months, was lost the day before yesterday. The grounds for the decision were that forcible feeding was necessary to save Miss Leigh's life. It was also stated that only the most minimal force was used. This means that the Home Secretary is within his rights to order the feeding of every woman prisoner who chooses hunger strike as a last means of protest.

Mrs Pankhurst is required to pay the court costs or face prison herself. She learned of this judgement as she disembarked from the ship that had returned her from a successful lecture tour of America. What a terrible welcome home!

12th December 1909

An unknown supporter has paid Mrs Pankhurst's fine. That is cheering, but I hoped that we would have so much more to celebrate by this year's end.

I must be positive! Mother's health is greatly improved and that is cause for celebration. She looked blooming this evening.

Celia Loverton told me today that she lives with her grandmother because her parents are in India. Her father is employed by the British Consulate in Delhi, and they are not coming home for the holidays.

14th December 1909

Everyone is preparing for a General Election early
next year. There is hope that the Tories might win. My
choice is Mr Hardie and the Labour Party, but the
important thing is to oust this anti-suffrage lot!

15th December 1909

It has been snowing! I built a snowman in the yard
and then Flora and I had great fun hanging Christmas
decorations. She has invited Mother here for the
festivities but Mother says she wouldn't feel at ease.
These are the occasions when I feel torn between my
two worlds.

I asked Celia where she feels she belongs.

"With grandmama, I suppose," she told me. "I rarely
see my parents."

18th December 1909

We had a jolly "Bloomsbury Christmas Party" yesterday evening. Several of Flora's friends came over for supper. Among them were Cicely Hamilton, actress and novelist, Elizabeth Robins, who is writing now, and the Irishman, George Bernard Shaw – gosh, he's brilliant! Their conversation was of plans to form a Women Writers' Suffrage League. It is to be fronted by some of the most eminent literary figures of today, men as well as women. The idea would be to support all suffrage leagues, whether militant or constitutional. It's so exciting. Flora is right behind it, too.

"You see, Dollie," she said, kissing me goodnight. "We can win this battle with intellect and not aggression."

I wish I could believe her!

26th December 1909

It has been a splendid Christmas. Yesterday morning I went to the hospital to visit Mother. All my brothers and their families were there. I wanted to run off, but of course I didn't and everything was fine. We all got on quite well and Mother looked really relaxed.

"All my families together in one place," she laughed.

Today, Celia came over for lunch. We had turkey and steaming baked potatoes and then talked in my room for ages. She told me all about her parents in Delhi and how much she misses them. She is really nice. I think we might have more in common than I supposed.

3rd January 1910

According to the New Year issue of *Votes for Women*, working-class suffrage prisoners are being treated far worse than their more privileged sisters. Reading such articles reassures me that I am right to fight with the WSPU.

24th January 1910

Saw Mother. She looked well and wanted to know what I have been up to. I told her all about Lady Constance Lytton who was in prison last year and who was released after two days of hunger strike without being force-fed. "She believes that she was treated with compassion because she is an aristocrat."

Mother frowned. "She probably was, but who cares about toffs like her?"

"She cares about us," I replied.

"Oh, yeah?" she scoffed.

"This year she returned to prison under the name of 'Jane Wharton', went on hunger strike and was force-fed on numerous occasions before her true identity was discovered. Yesterday she was released from prison. She has been giving interviews to the press. Her story has scandalized the nation."

"People of our class have no rights, Dollie. I don't have to be thrown in prison to learn that. It's why I want you to do good at your school and stop this nonsense."

"I do work at school but I also know that I have to fight for women's rights and that MUST include the interests of working-class women. Think, if you could read and write —"

"Keep your voice down," she snapped. "You'll wake the old girl in the next bed. You've the chance to rise above the abyss, Dollie. Grab it. Stop fussing about the rest of it. Fight for yourself."

Sometimes I think she'll never understand how much this matters to me, and why.

31st January 1910

A committee has been formed to draft a parliamentary bill. It will be known as the Conciliation Committee Women's Franchise Bill and, *if passed*, will offer voting rights to property-owning women. Married women and working-class women, which would include me if I were old enough and my mother, will still not be eligible to vote. The reasoning is that if we fight for all women, no one will get it.

I am disappointed by the narrowness of the Bill's draft because it goes against everything I want to see achieved, but Mrs Pankhurst and Christabel feel that our only chance is to win our rights by degrees. I trust them, so I will back them.

In order to help the Bill gain parliamentary support, Mrs Pankhurst has called a truce on all militant acts. We, the members of the WSPU, have agreed to uphold this. We will continue to lobby vociferously but without militancy.

Flora has declared the truce an excellent move. I do not agree with her. I am incensed by the treatment of suffrage prisoners, particularly those of my own class, who are suffering far greater measures of cruelty. But our debate on these issues today was friendly.

14th February 1910

I can hardly believe it! The Liberals have won the election, with the support of the Labour party. Perhaps this will force them to take notice of the women's issue.

Celia told me that her grandmother doesn't want her to get involved with any political organizations. I tried to persuade her just to come along and hear what it's all about, but she said she didn't dare go against her grandmother.

20th February 1910

I believe Mrs Pankhurst is also troubled by the fact that this bill is so narrow, but she is keeping quiet because she does not want to upset the apple cart. She is determined that, one way or another, a bill will go through. Her policy is to think practically. Once the vote has been won for a few women, it will pave the way for the rest of us. If it goes through I shan't cheer too loudly because ALL WOMEN OF EIGHTEEN AND OLDER should be allowed to vote.

17th April 1910

Mother has been released from hospital! At last! I went in a hansom to collect her and we travelled back to the East End together.

"Please stay a while at Flora's?" I begged as we approached the slums.

She shook her head.

"You have nothing to worry about," I assured her. I reminded her of the money I shall receive when I am 21, and I promised, as I always do, that I will look after her. I offered again to move her to comfortable lodgings.

Her response was a shrug. "This is where I belong," she answered.

At least my brothers were there to greet her and welcome her home. But I left feeling troubled.

7th May 1910

The most unexpected news yesterday was the death of our king, Edward VII. He was not a supporter of our work and some say that he positively encouraged the government's decision to begin force-feeding, so I do not feel a great desire to mourn.

Visited Mother. She seems settled back at home but it worries me that the lack of comfort will make her sick again.

20th May 1910

As a mark of respect for the King, the mammoth peaceful suffrage demonstration that had been scheduled for the 28th of this month has been postponed until Sunday 18th June.

Saw Mother today. She was in one of her difficult moods. I think I grew over-enthusiastic again about my work with the WSPU. She retorted with dismissives about what she describes as "the crowd" I am involved with.

"Education has got you nowhere, my girl," she said to me. "Out in the streets with banners, ranting and raving about women's rights. I don't know what fancy notions have got into that head of yours. A woman's place is in the home with her family."

I sighed and attempted to explain again. "You were the one who sent me away. You were the one who thought that an education would give me opportunities."

"Yes, but I didn't think it would fill your head with all this nonsense and make you dress la-di-da. I hope you're not getting yourself into trouble with all your talk about women in prison. If I thought..."

"I am fighting for you!"

"But what's the point, Dollie? I don't vote."

"Because you don't have the right to, Mother."

"But even if I did, I wouldn't. What damned difference would it make to the likes of me? Poor is poor, whoever is running the show."

"Not necessarily! Think how different your life might have been if you had been offered an opportunity to study. If you could have earned your own living and not been forced to rely on Father. I know what he put you through," I said. "If you had been independent you could have chosen to leave." It is the first time I have ever dared to broach the subject and she pounced on me like a reptile after a fly.

"You watch your mouth, my girl! I won't hear a word said against your father in this house."

It was plain how she still misses him, though he has been dead for over six years now. Whenever I visit, she talks of him. "The life of a docker, the stresses and the booze sent him to an early grave. Just past 40-years old, he was, when he died. He was a good man," she says, more to herself than to me.

And so to change the subject and because it was

almost time for me to leave, I stroked her cheek and said, "Next time I visit I would like to invite Flora, if you will welcome her. She has expressed a desire to see you again. May I?"

"You'll do as you will, whatever I say. You have high-class attitudes and think you know better than your own family, but if she wants to come then I'll not stop her."

"And perhaps you might consider coming to the West End and visiting us."

"Not bleedin' likely! And have all them posh Bonnington folk saying, 'She's not one of us.' No, I know my place, thanks all the same, Dollie. But yer a good girl. You're bright and I'm proud of yer."

I nearly fell over. She has never complimented me like that before.

14th June 1910

Great good news! At last the Bill is to be debated in the Commons. It will make Sunday's march an upbeat affair. I have persuaded Mother to accompany us.

"It's only to see," she said. "And to stop yer nagging me about not knowin' what's what."

I am so looking forward to sharing such an important part of my life with her. Celia has agreed to come along too.

"What about your grandmama?" I asked her, but she assured me that her grandmother sees it as a harmless "bit of fun" and a celebration of the new king.

18th June 1910

We marched from the Embankment to the Albert Hall. It was a glorious day. The sun shone warmly. Everyone was in good spirits. More than 10,000 people had come from all over the world and there were dozens of bands playing. It was incredible. Even Mother looked happy, she who has been so opposed to my involvement with the WSPU. I think the fact she agreed to march with us pleased me more than anything else. Her face was full of wonder. I had to take good care of her, though, so that the press of people did not harm her. She is still so frail.

I introduced her to Miss Baker and to Mary Richardson, and all of them to Celia. They were all lovely to Mother. We read some of the slogans aloud because she couldn't read them for herself.

We waved banners, carried flowers, sang along with the tunes. Hundreds who have been imprisoned for our cause marched together in a powerful band. It was all very rousing to the spirit. I felt proud to be a woman, proud to be alive, proud to be a part of a movement that is fighting to make a difference.

When we arrived at the Albert Hall, Mrs Pankhurst rose to speak first. Cheers rang out from all around us. She opened with the statement: "One word: Victory!" And then she read an address calling upon the government to grant facilities for the Women's Suffrage Bill before the end of the summer session.

The crowds cheered her once again and laughed and shouted.

"Gosh, I can see why you're so enthusiastic," Celia shouted to me through the din. "Your friend, Miss Baker, has offered to tell me all about what's going on, and I think I should be involved."

I was so glad she wasn't disappointed.

Then a collection was taken for the Cause.

"Is that her then?" my mother asked. "Is that yer famous leader?"

I nodded. "What do you think?"

"Well, she's distinguished and she's got a way with words, I grant you that."

And I knew then that Mother was on her way to being won over. I stood watching as she gazed all around her, taking it all in, with astonishment. Her eyes were bright as round blue buttons. "I thought it'd be a load of toffs," she murmured, "but it's a real mixed bag, all right. See over there."

I turned to where she was pointing and saw a gaggle of young women giggling and chattering together.

"Them's a bunch of seamstresses from the East End. I 'eard 'em talking back near that Marbled Arch." She smiled at me and we hugged one another tight.

A sea of women, and men too, rallying for a new future. It seemed to me as though we could taste victory this afternoon.

19th June 1910

The procession of yesterday was two miles long and the collection raised £5,000 for the WSPU campaign. We are all quite staggered and exhilarated.

Mother was exhausted by the time I got her home last night, but admitted to having enjoyed it much more than she had expected.

I'll make a suffragette of her yet!

12th July 1910

The Bill has passed its second reading in the House today with an excellent majority of 109. Not surprisingly, both our Prime Minister, Mr Asquith, and his Chancellor of the Exchequer, Mr Lloyd George, voted against it! And Mr Churchill has also voted against it. If that does not prove how anti-suffrage the leaders of this country are, I don't know what does. But with a healthy majority, we can still get this bill made law.

School broke up for the summer today. I invited Celia to the rally next week, but her parents have just arrived from India and they are taking her to Italy for six weeks. "But I will come again," she promised. "It was great fun last time."

23rd July 1910

Another splendid rally today, out under the blazing-hot sun. This time the march took us to Hyde Park. There must have been close to a quarter of a million people present. There were Men's Leagues and Women's Leagues from all over the world, banners in every direction brilliantly displaying our Union colours and large signs inscribed with the word *Justice*. Flora and Elizabeth Robins led the Actresses' Franchise League.

Everything remained peaceful and people are sticking to the truce, but there was an air of restlessness and concern. Asquith is creating obstacles for the Bill; he is stalling for time. Many believe that these are tricks of his to block the Bill's hearing before the end of the summer session.

24th July 1910

I was at Clements Inn this morning when I heard the news. Asquith has announced that the Conciliation Bill will be given no more time this session. This means that, at the very earliest, we must wait until the House reconvenes in the autumn.

Everyone was bitterly disappointed. Emily Wilding Davison, a brilliant woman and one of our most militant and devoted members, and Mary Richardson were among those who called for the truce to be lifted and a return to militant acts of demonstration, but Mrs Pankhurst said no. "Let us wait and see what happens in the autumn."

So even the most extreme among us have agreed to wait, but it is deeply frustrating.

The offices will operate for most of August with only a skeleton staff because many of the women, including Mrs Pankhurst, are going away. I have agreed to lend a hand.

30th July 1910

Flora has been trying to persuade me to go travelling with her. Part of me would enjoy it, but I refused. I feel I should stay in London and be close to my mother, and I want to keep my promise to help staff the WSPU offices.

12th August 1910

London feels quite empty already and I am rather lonely, but I have managed to catch up on a heap of school reading. Once the vote is through I will need to concentrate on taking my exams and getting into university. So these long-drawn-out days have a useful purpose.

I took the bus over to see Mother this evening. I came up with the most wonderful plan and can't think why I haven't thought of it sooner. I could teach her to read and write. But when I suggested it, she shook her head. "It's too late for all that, Dollie."

"It's never too late," I retorted, but she refused to discuss the matter further. There are days when she infuriates me.

23rd August 1910

Miss Baker returned from visiting her family yesterday. This afternoon we walked in sunny Green Park together and caught up on all our news.

A postcard arrived from Flora saying that she will be back by the middle of September.

18th October 1910

Flora gave a party at the house this evening in honour of her friend, Edward Morgan Forster, who published his new novel today. He is a writer I enjoy. Or, to be truthful, although he has published three previous works I have only so far read his last, *A Room With a View*, which was great fun. Much of it is set in Italy, a country loved by my dearly missed patron, Lady Violet. But I did not attend the *soirée* because I spent the evening at the Union offices. Everyone is agitated about what will happen when Parliament reconvenes. Mrs Pankhurst has written to Mr Asquith to forewarn him that if no time is made for our bill then militant demonstrations will recommence.

10th November 1910

Flora burst into my room this morning with a mountain of lovely gifts for me. A silk kimono from Japan, embroidered Indian slippers, French cologne and Forster's latest novel, *Howard's End*. Apparently, it is causing quite a stir. "Edward has written a dedication to you and here, look, I cut out this splendid review from the most recent issue of *The Spectator*."

I was rather overwhelmed by it all.

"I hope you like his book. I devoured it at one sitting and believe it quite excellent. You look tired, Dollie. You never stop studying. How is it going?" But she did not wait for my response. "Have a splendid birthday, my dearest." And she was gone to have her bath.

It's true; I have been swotting late into the night. I need to create as much free time as possible to devote to my Union duties. This is a critical time for us, as we await the news. After school, I attended a big meeting at the Albert Hall in support of the Conciliation Bill. £9,000 was raised. Wonderful! Emmeline in her address to the crowds said that if the Bill, in spite of our efforts, is thrown out by the government, then it will be the end of our truce.

Flora made me delicious hot chocolate when I arrived home. "You look frozen, dear. Have you had a lovely birthday?"

I thanked her again for my presents.

"Were you at the Albert Hall?"

I nodded, but did not elaborate.

"It is not my place to tell you what or what not to do, but your involvement troubles me. You know that, don't you, Dollie? If the Bill does not go through, I fear trouble from the militants."

12th November 1910

Mrs Pankhurst is reminding Mr Asquith regularly that Parliament must set aside time for the Conciliation Bill. There has been absolutely no assurance from him that this will happen, so she has called upon members to mass together on the 18th for a special deputation. The march is to coincide with the reassembling of Parliament.

I will have to skip school to be there.

14th November 1910

I confided in Celia today that I won't be at school on Friday. When I explained why she expressed a wish to march. "I haven't dared join the WSPU yet, but being there will be like creating modern history."

18th November 1910

Celia and I met outside the tube station at Tottenham Court Road.

"I brought sandwiches," she said. "Isn't this exciting? I've never played truant before."

Arriving at Caxton Hall we found a crowd of several hundred women. "There has been bad news," Ada Wright informed the members.

Then Emmeline, with Christabel at her side, rose to speak.

"Earlier this morning, Mr Asquith opened his first parliamentary session by informing the Commons that negotiations with the House of Lords have broken down and Parliament is to be dissolved by the King on 28th November. He went on to say that between now and that date, priority will be given to government business. No mention whatsoever has been made of our conciliation bill."

Cries of disappointment and anger rang through the crowds. Mrs Pankhurst held her hands high, requesting silence. She then made it plain that, in spite of this news, the demonstration was to be peaceful. "I will deliver the following Memorial to our Prime Minister, and we will make our point. But there are to be no acts of militancy." She read out to us the Memorial she had been intending to give to Asquith:

This meeting of women, gathered together in the Caxton Hall, protests against the policy of shuffling and delay with which the agitation for women's enfranchisement has been met by the government, and calls on the government at once to withdraw the veto which they have placed upon the Conciliation Bill for Women's Suffrage, a measure which has been endorsed by the representatives of the people in the House of Commons.

There was general cheering and support and then, led by Emmeline, Christabel and Elizabeth Garrett Anderson, about 300 of us, including Mary Richardson, Ada Wright, Miss Baker, Celia and myself, marched from Caxton Hall to Parliament. Although determined in our purpose, we were all good-humoured. We walked in bands of twelve or sixteen, many arm in arm. Celia ate one of her sandwiches, offering me the other, but I was nervous and not hungry. All was harmonious and pleasant until we reached the steps of the House of Commons. There we found lines of police waiting for us, and our mood immediately darkened. I heard later that many of the bobbies had been brought in specially by the new Home Secretary, Mr Winston Churchill, from the district of Whitechapel (where they are used to rough work).

Before any of us could reach the House of Commons we had to face organized gangs of both plain-clothes police and those in uniform. Suddenly, as we moved forward, they began to shove, push and accost us. Some women got frightened and began to scream. Celia was one. I saw her panic, turning in circles. It was horrible. Friends all around me were being hurt. Celia was manhandled by a bobby. She screamed hysterically. I tried to reach her but it was chaotic. I couldn't get through the press of people. Men shoving, women being pushed. Then I felt a hard blow against the base of my neck and fell to the ground. A man's boot kicked me in the ribs. A hand hauled me to my feet again.

By that time Mrs Pankhurst and Mrs Garrett Anderson had got through, but I had lost all sight of Celia and I was scared for her. Several policemen a few feet away from me began tearing women's clothes, touching them in improper places. Foul words were spoken. I was very afraid and deeply shocked. I yelled out, "Celia!" but it was hopeless. I began to feel sick.

Though trembling, I moved on forward alongside Ada and 50 or so others until we reached the steps. As we did so we were forced back by the police. It was like a human wall pressing against us.

A female voice I didn't recognize called out: "This way! Follow me."

A small band of us turned left. We were to enter the House by an underground passage that was known to some, though not to me. Unfortunately the police pursued us and the scene that followed was ghastly. We were attacked and, in certain cases, sexually molested by members of the police force. Their manners and their tongues were brutal and indecent. I cannot even write the words I heard spoken by those men. I myself was grabbed by the hair and dragged back out on to the street where I was pushed until my knees buckled and I dropped to the ground on all fours like an animal. Even then I was beaten hard. I was not arrested but kicked back into a jeering crowd, bleeding and bruised.

I made my way back to Bloomsbury alone. My clothes hung from me like rags, my legs were sore and I was fighting back tears. Fortunately, Flora was out when I arrived home. I would not have wanted her to see the condition I was in, nor to know that I had not attended school. I dread to think what Celia's grandmother will say if she has arrived home in a similar condition.

19th November 1910

A photograph printed in this morning's *Daily Mirror* shows Ada Wright thrown to the ground, beaten and hurt. The paper headlined yesterday's incidents "Black Friday", and so we will christen the day. The number of women arrested is recorded as well over 100. And at least 50 women were seriously injured. How is it possible that our police could behave in such a disgusting way?

I am covered in scratches and bruises and had horrid nightmares. Thank Heaven it is Saturday and there is no school, except that there is no news from Celia.

I skipped breakfast and avoided Flora all day. If she had seen me and guessed where I had been, she would have been furious.

22nd November 1910

No one has even mentioned my absence from school, but there is an uproar about Celia who was arrested on Friday. Apparently her grandmother was summoned to the police station and, after various formalities, Celia was released without being charged, because of her age.

She looked pale today and she has several cuts on her face. "I didn't mention you," she whispered at break. "There was no point in getting us both into trouble. I have been forbidden any involvement in suffrage activities. My grandmother says I have acted like a hooligan and disgraced the family name."

"But you haven't! What happened on Friday wasn't your fault. It was a peaceful demonstration until the police became aggressive."

"I know, even so..."

"Thank you," I said, and I hugged her because I thought she was going to cry and because I feel horribly guilty about her.

14th December 1910

The weather is endlessly wet which seems to more than match the mood of these days. The police are claiming that it was not they who touched women indecently on Black Friday. A report from the Commissioner of the Metropolitan Police denies all accusations.

Mr Churchill has stated that the only ones to blame for the disagreeable scenes on 18th November were the "disorderly women themselves". What a truly horrid man he is!

17th December 1910

School broke up today. Celia told me that she won't be coming back next term. Her parents are returning to India and she must either go with them or be sent to a boarding school outside London.

Life feels grim. We are about to face our second General Election within a year.

20th December 1910

Asquith has been returned to power. Again! Oh, why could we not have been given lovely Mr Keir Hardie, along with his colleague George Lansbury? They and certain others in the Labour Party are so much more sympathetic to our cause. Asquith's majority remains very small so I must take heart from that.

Flora's father, Sir Thomas Bonnington, was here. I was on my way out of the door to see my mother when he arrived. Obviously, Flora introduced me. I nodded and then hurried away as soon as I could. He is an old man now but there was a look in his eyes that made me shiver. My father used to speak of him as cold and heartless. Seeing him today, I understand why.

27th December 1910

Flora told me this morning that Mrs Pankhurst's sister, Mary Clarke, died quite suddenly on Christmas Day. She had been released from prison only two days earlier. I wonder what part the shocking conditions of prison life have played in her unexpected death? I am typing a condolence letter.

(I mustn't boast, but my typing is rather skilled now. I love Flora for buying me such a present.)

20th January 1911

At the WSPU offices there is talk that Christabel and Mrs Pankhurst will renew the truce. Although a great number of the members are pressing to return to militancy, the Pankhursts are holding them back. The organization is in dispute. There are many who feel that we have been betrayed too many times already – I am one of them! – and then there are those, loyal to the Pankhursts, who will follow their leaders' advice whatever. Others say Mrs Pankhurst is tired and sad. During this last year she has lost her only son, her mother and now her sister. Certain members feel that she wants peace at any price and an end to this interminable suffrage struggle.

Emily Wilding Davison asked me if I was sufficiently passionate about winning the vote that I would die for it. I couldn't immediately answer.

"The Cause needs a martyr," she said.

Suddenly I pictured Celia Loverton with her cut face. She, in a modest way, has become a sort of martyr to me. She is probably on the boat to India now. I miss her.

Others may feel as strongly as Emily obviously does. The overruling sentiment within the WSPU is that this government is deaf to our pleas and "it is time to go to battle". It is certainly what I feel.

21st January 1911

Flora took me to a concert this evening. It was a celebration for released prisoners. The music, *The March of the Women*, had been written especially for the event.

6th February 1911

Our new government has met for the first time. There is a move towards a new bill for us, a Second Conciliation Bill, though no mention was made of it in the King's speech.

15th March 1911

Serious criticism is being lobbied against our organization, of Mrs Pankhurst and Christabel, too. It hurts to read it, and I believe it confuses the general public. Even within the WSPU, disputes and alliances are dividing us. We should not fight among ourselves. It is important that our goal bonds us. Miss Baker assures me that Mrs Pankhurst is aware of the situation, but accepts that within any organization divisions and struggles are inevitable. It seems wrong to me.

16th March 1911

The Second Conciliation Bill is due to have its first reading on 5th May. Again it is disappointing because, as with the first, *if* it goes through, it will only allow the vote to women who are householders. The argument remains the same: its narrowness will secure its success.

Mrs Pankhurst has a new car. It is a Wolseley and jolly smart. She has her own driver, too – a woman, and the first to be admitted to the Automobile Association. Well, that is a move in a good direction, I suppose.

When my inheritance is paid, I might buy myself a car. I won't have a chauffeur, though. I rather fancy being at the wheel. I will be able to take Mother out, too. Anything to get her out of that horrid area.

19th March 1911

A national Census is due to be taken on 2nd April.

A boycott has been planned by all the various women's groups, constitutionalists and militants alike. Instead of completing the form, the recommended response, written boldly across it, is, "No vote. No Census."

It's an excellent idea. It appeals to Flora, too, and her passive approach. *The Times*, of course, has criticized us.

20th March 1911

Over breakfast this morning, Flora read aloud Mrs Pankhurst's reply to *The Times*, which is terrific!

"The Census is a numbering of people. Until women count as people for the purpose of representation in the councils of the nation as well as for the purposes of taxation and of obedience to the laws, we advise women to refuse to be numbered."

YES!

"What will you write on our household form, Flora?" I asked.

She laughed at my earnestness. "If Mr Asquith has not pledged, on or before the beginning of April, to allow women's suffrage I shall do as Millicent, Emmeline and Christabel and like-minded suffragists are advising. I shall write in large letters right across our form: No Vote. No Census. There, Dollie, does that please you?"

"Perfectly!" I cried.

3rd April 1911

I am EXHAUSTED. Last night was Census night.

No pledge had been forthcoming from horrible Asquith, so suffrage supporters held an all-night vigil. Flora and I attended a concert organized by the WSPU at the Queen's Hall (where the Exhibition was held two years ago). Afterwards, about 1,000 of us walked around Trafalgar Square in a circular procession for ages. It was magnificent. Everyone was so united. And then we went to the Scala Theatre, where there was entertainment until three in the morning. I have never been up so late before. Flora performed a pro-suffrage poem. What a splendid actress she is! After that, many of the supporters went on to the Aldwych Skating Rink for all-night skating, but we returned home. We walked all the way to Bloomsbury in the cold air, arms linked. Passers-by, who were nothing to do with us, waved and shouted their support. Even a few bobbies called out, "Good on yer!"

We stopped at an all-night café for mugs of scalding-hot tea and sticky buns.

"Your performance tonight was great, Flora. I would have loved my mother to have heard you," I said as we walked on.

"Thank you. Yes, I was surprised when you said she wasn't coming."

"She's been sick again. It's nothing serious but she does have to take care. I wish she'd leave that cottage. The damp gets in to her bones. But she seems happy and John is kind to her, even if he thinks I have become a 'stuck-up missie'. Lord, Flora, I hope I haven't."

Flora roared with laughter and hugged me tight. We were shivering with cold. "Is that why you are so passionate about all this?" she asked softly. "Is it all for your mother?"

"Maybe," I answered, but I wasn't able to explain more. It's funny; even after all this time I have never been able to open up to Flora about what drives me to this work. The only person to whom I ever confided the terrors of my childhood was Lady Violet.

The fact is that everything I am fighting for, the women's battle I am committed to, is fuelled by memories that will always haunt me. Those nights when Father came home drunk or deadbeat or out of work and took his moods and frustrations out on my mother. Sometimes he would hit her and those nights were the worst. I would lie in my bed, wanting to die. Sometimes I would get up and rush at him and beg him to stop, tears streaming down my face, but then he would turn on me, too.

I would lie awake listening to her sobbing and it devastated me that there was nothing I could do for her. Nothing that she could do for herself. Yet, even today, I do not believe that Father was a cruel man. My parents were caught up in a situation that they could not get free of.

My mother has sacrificed her life for him and the family. But I ask myself how it would have been if she had been educated and could have found independence, if she had not been financially dependent on him. Or how might it have been for him if she could have carried the financial load with him? What shame did he suffer knowing he could not feed his family?

4th April 1911

The news is that all across the country supporters held the all-night vigil to boycott the Census. A large midnight feast took place on Wimbledon Common where they tucked into roasted fowl, boiled ham, coffee and lashings of hot tea. What a fun way to protest!

Emily Wilding Davison hid herself in the Houses of Parliament. It had been her intention to rush into the House first thing on Monday when the Prime Minister appeared and shout, "Mr Asquith, withdraw your veto from the Women's Bill and women will withdraw their veto from the Census." Unfortunately, she was found by a cleaner in the crypt of St Stephen's Chapel. The police were called but she was not charged, though her name has been added to the Census numbers.

How daring, to stay there alone in the dark. I would have been absolutely petrified.

23rd April 1911

There was a meeting at the Queen's Hall this evening, which I missed because I had a mass of homework to catch up on. I heard later that Mrs Pankhurst gave a rip-roaring speech which finished with: "We believe that this cause of the emancipation of women is not only the greatest cause in the 20th century, but we believe it is also the most urgent and the most necessary."

Yes! It reminded me of Celia saying, "We are making modern history." I miss her.

5th May 1911

The revised Conciliation Bill passed its second reading in the House of Commons today with a truly excellent majority – 88 votes against and 255 in favour.

It looks as though, AT LAST, a handful of women are soon to win the vote.

The news was announced at a mammoth meeting at Kensington Town Hall, which Flora and I attended together. She accompanies me when she feels that the mood is determined but peaceable. I love it when she's there; it forms a bond between us.

Let's work as we have never worked before to get this bill passed during this session of parliament. That was the gist of Mrs Pankhurst's call to us all. Our cheers must have been audible all the way to Hyde Park.

Afterwards Miss Baker, Flora and I were invited to dinner with Emmeline Pethwick-Lawrence and her husband, Frederick. Their house is terribly posh but they are really nice and very generous and so committed to Christabel and Mrs Pankhurst and the Cause. Flora and Miss Baker started up a heated but friendly debate during the meal about the continuation or not of the present truce against militant action. Miss Baker and I were the two who most favour militancy. The Pethwick-Lawrences counselled caution and Flora remains firmly against it.

29th May 1911

Mr Lloyd George confirmed in the Commons today that Mr Asquith will make no time for a second reading of the Second Conciliation Bill this session. It will have to wait until 1912.

I hate those politicians. We have been cheated. This could end the militancy truce and might well affect the King's Coronation procession next month.

12th June 1911

Christabel informed a large gathering of us at the office last night that she has received sound reassurance that at next year's session our bill will be given all the time it requires to make certain of its successful passage. I think this news, coming from her, who would normally countenance militancy, has quietened the angry hearts of a few. Personally, I cannot help asking myself why the promises always remain somewhere far-off in the distant future.

17th June 1911

A stupendous procession took place today, which, although sponsored by us, was supported by 28 other suffrage groups. We named it the Women's Coronation Procession. It was the best ever. All the various suffrage groups united, and it went off without any violent incidents.

It began at the Embankment. Everyone walked seven abreast or rode on horseback – horses had been loaned to us by supporters everywhere. I spotted a chestnut mare eating the daisies off the straw hat of a girl in the crowd lining the pavements. When I pointed it out, my row got the giggles.

It was a cold, bright day but the exercise kept us warm. As we approached Piccadilly there were roaring salutes and cheers. I was puzzled. Then I spied an old lady sitting on a balcony, decked out in our colours. An inscription on the railing read: *The Oldest Militant Suffragette Greets You.* I couldn't believe my eyes. It was Elizabeth Wolstenholme Elmy. She has been a fighter for our cause for the past 50 years and was a great friend of Lady Violet's.

It brought home to me for how long and tirelessly women have been fighting for the right to be acknowledged as the equals of men.

22nd June 1911

Today was the official Coronation day. The crowning of King George V. In my opinion it was a shadow of our spectacular Women's Coronation Parade last Saturday; everybody is still talking about the immense support we received. Our procession was seven miles long!

24th August 1911

A very worrying article has appeared in the latest issue of our *Votes for Women* newspaper (which I am no longer selling because Harriet Kerr has promoted me to a summer typing job). It states that Lloyd George, speaking on behalf of the Prime Minister, has broken faith with the Conciliation Committee by suggesting that another bill of a similar nature could be given facilities next session. Our journal states that if he betrays women's suffrage societies, the WSPU will "revert to a state of war".

Mrs Pankhurst is away so we have not yet received her opinion. I haven't quite understood the implications. Harriet sincerely hopes that we won't be forced back to aggressive tactics. Christabel warns that we must be wary of Lloyd George, that he is an enemy of women's suffrage.

The problem seems to be that Lloyd George wants the Conciliation Bill to offer voting eligibility to a broader band of women. On the face of it, that sounds splendid. However, Miss Baker advises that this would almost certainly lead to the Bill's defeat. "The Liberals are terrified. Women all over the country have campaigned tirelessly against them because they have refused to give us suffrage rights. If this bill goes through, they know that every woman with a voice will vote against them and they will lose the next election. So, they have no intention of making it law."

7th November 1911

Asquith has announced that a Manhood Suffrage Bill, which would give the vote to a wider section of the male population, is to be introduced into the next session. The Bill will allow for an amendment, if the House of Commons supports it, for certain classes of women to be enfranchised.

Christabel has cabled the news to her mother, who left for the United States a month ago on a speaking tour.

We have been betrayed!

10th November 1911

It is my birthday. I went and had tea with my mother. Two of my brothers and their families were present. One of them took me aside and ticked me off, saying that I caused my mother "nothing but worry with all your talk about women's rights".

I was speechless. I was sure Mother was beginning to support us.

12th November 1911

News from Mrs Pankhurst in the States affirms new and more militant activities. Christabel has announced that the WSPU is returning to an anti-government policy.

Flora was most upset when I told her this evening. "It will do you no good getting involved with illegal acts. You must think of your education and your future."

"It is no future," I rejoined, "if I grow up into a world where women are not recognized as citizens and are not free to follow the professions they choose. A world where the majority of them cannot read, write or earn their keep."

17th November 1911

A deputation, led by Christabel and Mrs Pethwick-Lawrence, of nine suffrage societies, including the Actresses' Franchise League, was received by Asquith today, but he stressed that women's suffrage will not become a government measure while he is in power. The only path he will follow is the Manhood Suffrage Bill.

Flora was very depressed when she returned this evening, but she still maintains that militancy is not the direction. I DISAGREED WITH HER! We had a horrid argument and here I am in bed, writing my diary, feeling upset.

18th November 1911

The WSPU has issued an official statement. Hostilities are to be resumed.

21st November 1911

Mrs Pethwick-Lawrence led a march from Caxton Hall to the House of Commons today. I did not participate because I accompanied a smaller group of other militant friends, including Miss Baker. Armed with bags and pockets laden with stones – some of us had hammers – we smashed the windows of several city-centre stores. I broke the glass of two windows of Lyons' Tea Shop. Swan & Edgar, the department store, was damaged, as was Dunn's Hat Shop.

Others targeted newspaper offices, the *Daily Mail* and *Daily News*, while several men's clubs came under attack.

Over 200 were arrested, including Mrs Pethwick-Lawrence and Mary Leigh. I was caught, too, but when the bobby learned my age he let me go and I legged it home. I said nothing to Flora. She'd be livid if she knew. I have never indulged in illegal deeds before and I am shaken by the force of my anger today. Also, I have a deepish cut between my wrist and my left thumb. Still, I don't regret my actions. This has to be done.

23rd November 1911

At the Savoy Hotel this evening, Christabel publicly defended the violence of two days ago. She claims that men won their right to vote through riot and rebellion and we must do the same.

Flora interrogated me about my bandaged hand, and I lied to her. Oh, Lord. I think fibbing to her – she who is practically my sister – hurts more than anything. But what choice do I have?

28th November 1911

Many feel that the "vandalism" was inappropriate because it was carried out against *private* property, not public. The movement has never previously targeted personal possessions.

Christabel maintains that such acts may need to be repeated.

Flora is absolutely furious. She made me promise not to get involved. It was awful, making a promise I knew I would be obliged to break. I am in full support of more extreme acts, but I hate the deceit this is forcing me into.

4th December 1911

Mr Lloyd George has been publicly boasting that he has "torpedoed the Conciliation Bill". Horrid man. I want to torpedo him. It is no wonder that women's anger is reaching such a pitch of violence. The government betrays us and then gloats about it publicly.

Mrs Pankhurst might cut short her trip and sail back to fight with us, though we are well led by Christabel.

15th December 1911

Emily Wilding Davison soaked strips of linen with paraffin, lit them and then thrust them into various pillar-boxes today. Some of us found this all a bit shocking. I don't think her actions were sanctioned by the WSPU leaders. She was arrested near the Parliament Street post office and has been committed to trial at the Old Bailey.

Emily is convinced that the publicity will bring us new supporters. She believes that only once we express the depth of our commitment will the government and the country really take heed and fully comprehend what we are fighting for, and how profoundly important to mankind our cause is.

I spoke to Flora about Emily's thoughts. "She goes too far," was her response, "and that is why she is no longer employed by the WSPU."

"She is still a Union member," I retorted.

"But she acts alone. She is a renegade and that is dangerous."

I did not dare reply that I think Emily and others of a like mind will go to even greater lengths if they deem it necessary. Am I one of those? I cannot be sure, but I think so and that scares me.

13th January 1912

Emily Wilding Davison has been sentenced to SIX months' imprisonment. We are all reeling with shock at the severity of such a sentence.

22nd January 1912

Mrs Pankhurst has returned from the States. She spoke at the London Pavilion, declaring that she will support nothing less than a government bill of full sexual equality. She applauded us window-breakers of last November. If we are not given the opportunity to be heard then we must find other means to express our discontent.

We will fight this government and every succeeding one if it does not take up our cause, was her message.

1st March 1912

"Why should women go to Parliament Square and be battered about and insulted and, most important of all, produce less effect than when they throw stones? The argument of the broken pane of glass is the most valuable argument in modern politics."

Emmeline recently made this statement.

Today, led by her in Downing Street, women broke windows all over London.

Charlotte Marsh, Emily Wilding Davison's friend, who prefers to be called Charlie, and I shattered an entire row of shop windows in the Strand. Shards of glass lay like hundreds of puddles on the street behind us. We kept our hammers hidden in our muffs and walked fast. It was scary.

Approximately 150 women smashed 400 shop windows today. Mrs Pankhurst has been arrested for inciting violence. The total number arrested was around 120.

2nd March 1912

At Bow Street Magistrates' Court today Mrs Pankhurst was sentenced to two months' imprisonment in the THIRD DIVISION.

Her speech was amazing:

"If you send me to prison, as soon as I come out I will go further, to show that women who have to pay the salaries of Cabinet Ministers and who pay your salary too, Sir, are going to have some voice in the making of the laws which they have to obey."

3rd March 1912

Skipped school again – I haven't been in since last Thursday.

Both yesterday and today, groups of us have been out smashing windows again as a protest against Mrs Pankhurst's sentence. Many of the windows at Liberty's were broken.

Millicent Garret Fawcett spoke out against our militant acts and declared that the NUWSS stands where it has always stood.

Elizabeth Garrett Anderson has also condemned our violent behaviour and criticized Mrs Pankhurst.

4th March 1912

I was working at Clements Inn today when the police arrived, armed with a bunch of warrants. Both Mr and Mrs Pethwick-Lawrence were arrested. It was upsetting because Mrs P-L was only recently released from Holloway. Emmeline Pankhurst could not be arrested because she is already in prison, as is her comrade, Mabel Tuke. This left Christabel. A warrant was issued for her arrest, but she escaped.

Flora was telephoned. She agreed to give Christabel some contact addresses in Paris. The good news is that with Christabel still at liberty there is someone to direct the movement, even if it will be from a distance.

Annie Kenney, a great friend of Christabel's and the only working-class member of the WSPU leadership, says that we can continue to operate effectively. We must find a means of staying in contact with Christabel.

But the mood here is desperate. We feel cheated and betrayed.

7th March 1912

Flora is monumentally furious. The headmistress at St Paul's contacted her to find out where I have been. When she confronted me, I was forced to admit the truth. I can't keep deceiving her. Besides, I believe that what I am doing is right. VIOLENT PROTEST HAS TO BE MADE if we are to change the government's thinking.

"Why are you risking your future, which is so bright?" she shouted at me.

"Because without equal opportunities for women there is no future."

"But nothing justifies this violence, Dollie, nothing."

"It does, but you cannot understand because your life is comfortable and secure. You can work. You have money for food, even without the vote," I screamed back at her.

She was aghast. "Your fury reminds me of your mother when she turned up at our home during the dockers' strike. She was angry and abrasive, and refused to discuss anything with me and it got her nowhere."

How could I begin to explain to Flora about my mother's life or my early childhood memories? Never in a million years will she see my point of view. She has also forgotten that if my mother had not arrived unannounced at the Bonnington door Lady Violet would never have known about us, and I would not be here today, living this privileged life. So my mother's courage *did* make a difference.

"How far can you go for an ideal, Dollie? Think about it carefully, I beg you. What you have done is illegal. You could end up in prison, and then what will you have achieved?"

I left her and went to bed. I had no stamina left to fight with her, and besides it hurts me because I love her so much.

28th March 1912

A second reading was given to a barely revised Conciliation Bill and it has been rejected. I don't think our case has been served by an article in this morning's

Times, which stated that our revolutionary acts prove that we are all mentally unstable and not worthy of the vote.

Mrs Pankhurst and Mr and Mrs Pethwick-Lawrence have been committed for trial on charges of conspiracy, which means they are being charged with plotting to pervert the course of justice. That's really serious. Those who are left at Clements Inn are depressed. Our dreams of the vote for this year have been destroyed.

A massive turn-out tonight at the Albert Hall rallied to support our leaders and to show our defiance at the decisions taken by this turncoat Liberal government.

30th March 1912

Mrs Pankhurst has contracted bronchitis in her cell at Holloway and an appeal for bail has been refused. We fear for her fading health.

4th April 1912

Mrs Pankhurst has finally been released on medical grounds. Thank Heaven.

14th April 1912

Christabel is continuing to write columns for our paper, *Votes for Women*, but they are published anonymously. Annie Kenney makes weekly journeys across the Channel to get instructions for us from Christabel.

I am channelling my energies into my neglected school work and am deep in history and English essays. I have so much to catch up on!

15th May 1912

The conspiracy trial began at the Old Bailey today. All the newspapers are reporting on it, which gives a very high profile to our cause, even though the thought of Mrs Pankhurst being committed to prison for a long term makes me miserable.

22nd May 1912

Mrs Pankhurst made a very moving speech from the dock yesterday in which she pointed out again that we have been fighting for the vote since before the Reform Bill of 1867. It is despair and frustration that have driven women to such acts of militancy, she argued. She also talked of the appalling conditions in which so many women and children live. It stabbed at my heart.

But, despite her fine words, the all-male jury found Mrs Pankhurst, her friend Emmeline Pethwick-Lawrence and her husband Frederick guilty. They were sentenced to nine months in the Second Division and ordered to pay the prosecution costs of the trial. The women were taken back to Holloway and Mr Pethwick-Lawrence to Brixton prison.

NINE months in the SECOND DIVISION. How unjust can a system be!

1st June 1912

The prisoners have threatened to go on hunger strike unless they are given political status. Several Labour politicians, including George Lansbury and Keir Hardie, and hundreds of famous people, Flora and many of her friends included, are supporting this request.

It is encouraging to feel the public response.

10th June 1912

All three prisoners have been placed in the First Division. This is the first time the government has ever recognized our cause as a political one. It is a TRIUMPH!

14th June 1912

Our "triumph" was shortlived. It turns out that only the three leading suffrage prisoners are being granted political status. The others, some 78 prisoners, must stay in the Second or even Third Division cells. So, after all, it is not that the government recognizes our status; it is simply that they wish to appease the public outcry.

19th June 1912

A hunger strike began today. Emmeline and the Pethwick-Lawrences are supporting the rest of the movement and striking with them.

22nd June 1912

Doctors and nine wardresses entered Mrs Pethwick-Lawrence's cell today and forcibly fed her. Afterwards they flung open the door of Mrs Pankhurst's cell armed with force-feeding apparatus. Forewarned by the harrowing cries of Mrs Pethwick-Lawrence, she received them with all her anger and indignation, grabbed a large earthenware jug, held it above her head and said, "If any of you dares take so much as one step inside this cell I shall defend myself."

They fell back and left her. When she entered her friend's cell, she found her in a state of collapse.

26th June 1912

Mrs Pankhurst and Emmeline Pethwick-Lawrence have been released from Holloway, for health reasons.

Mrs Pankhurst spoke of the prison scenes that took place around her as "sickening and violent". She claims that "every hour of the day" she woke from nightmares and the doctors had to be called to calm her. During her imprisonment, she was assured that she would not be force-fed, but there are many other women still behind bars who are being subjected to this foul indignity.

Yesterday the Labour MP George Lansbury warned the Prime Minister in the House of Commons, "You will go down in history as the man who tortured innocent women."

1st July 1912

Mrs Pankhurst has left for Paris to visit Christabel, travelling under the name of "Mrs Richards". Before she left, Flora met her and gave her advice on various French matters, including medical care.

Although Flora deeply disagrees with the violent tactics we have used this year, she remains a great friend of Christabel's and holds Mrs Pankhurst in the highest esteem. When she returned home, she said that Mrs Pankhurst looked very frail and must take time off to rest.

4th July 1912

Emily Wilding Davison threw herself down an iron staircase in Holloway Prison last night. She was protesting against the treatment the prisoners have been receiving. I was told, but I don't know how accurate this is, that her intention was to kill herself. She wants to become the martyr she passionately believes our cause needs. She did not succeed because she fell upon some wire netting 30 feet below, but she was badly concussed and has severe injuries to her spine. She had to be seen by the prison doctors. Even so, today, she was forcibly fed again. I travelled to north London, to Holloway, to see her but I was refused a visit. It looks so grim in there. I was glad to get back on the bus.

10th July 1912

The Pethwick-Lawrences left for France. They are travelling to the Hotel de Paris in Boulogne where they will meet up with Christabel and her mother who are arriving from Paris. They intend to spend a few days together, recuperating. The hunger strikes have taken their toll.

17th July 1912

Confusing news has reached us at Clements Inn. It seems that there has been a disagreement between Emmeline and Christabel Pankhurst and the Pethwick-Lawrences. Mr and Mrs Pethwick-Lawrence have criticized the excessive violence our Union has resorted to and they were distressed to learn that the Pankhursts feel we must intensify our campaign, or all our work will have been to no avail. When they expressed their objections Mrs Pankhurst requested their *resignations* from the Union. This is incredible.

I cannot bear to think what this might mean. Could it be the beginning of the end? If the Union splits, will our fight have been in vain? I pray that they will find a way to resolve their differences. I wish I could talk to Miss Baker on this matter, but she, like so many of my friends, is in prison, and there is no point in pouring my heart out to Flora. She agrees with the Pethwick-Lawrences. Of course.

21st August 1912

We are in the throes of moving offices to Lincoln's Inn House. The chaos of files, pamphlets, papers and notes seems to me to reflect the state of affairs. I am exhausted from filling boxes and stacking crates and I feel angry and worn out by the government's cruelty and stubborn attitude.

25th August 1912

I have just learned that Christabel returned to London recently in disguise to meet Frederick and Emmeline Pethwick-Lawrence. She has confirmed that both she and her mother wish them to leave our organization. We are all quite stunned because they have been such loyal workers and have offered us so much financial support over the years.

When I got in this evening, Flora greeted me with, "I insist that you renounce all connections with the WSPU."

"You can't ask that," I retaliated.

"You must concentrate on your school work if you are to gain a place at university," was her argument.

My marks have been consistently high and I have been working extra hard so that I would not fall behind, for the precise reason that I have not wanted her to use my studies as an excuse to make me resign from the WSPU.

"Even if you throw me out on the street," I told her, "I won't give up this fight."

"Oh, Dollie, I will never throw you out, but I dread the thought of you ending up in prison. It's because I love you that I am begging you to find another way to channel your commitment."

"If you love me, Flora, please try to accept me for who I am," I replied and went upstairs to take a bath.

16th October 1912

We are just about installed at our new office address. The split with Mr and Mrs Pethwick-Lawrence is certain. They came to a meeting the other night at the offices and the matter was discussed openly. I am very sad because I like and respect them both. The members are very divided on this matter.

17th October 1912

Flora took me to the theatre to see a French actress, Sarah Bernhardt. She performed in Shakespeare's *The Winter's Tale* and was magnificent. Afterwards, we went backstage to her dressing room. Flora knows her rather well. It was incredibly exciting and I felt that it bonded Flora and me again after all our arguing and bickering during these last six weeks.

Elizabeth Robins was also in the audience. She was upset about the business with the Pethwick-Lawrences, but we did not discuss it in front of Flora.

18th October 1912

We have a new newspaper, *The Suffragette*. Its first issue appeared this morning. *Votes for Women* will be published by the Pethwick-Lawrences. They are continuing to support women's enfranchisement, but in their own, less militant, fashion.

Mrs Pankhurst's intentions for our future were stated clearly last night at a huge gathering at the Albert Hall, which I attended with Miss Baker who has just been released from prison. We are to show resistance not only to the government itself but also to the Irish and Labour parties who support the Liberal anti-suffrage policies.

Secret acts against public and private property, are what she counsels us to carry out. "Be militant in your own way," she said. "I incite this meeting to rebellion."

Flora, who has been spending time with the Pethwick-Lawrences, is horrified. She was mumbling something about sending me away to school. If she intends to, I shall run away.

24th November 1912

Mrs Pankhurst has been campaigning this month in the East End, in areas such as Bethnal Green and Limehouse. I have been accompanying her on several of these trips because I know the area a bit and because it is an aspect of the work that matters so deeply to me. Every time I hear her speak I feel the fire rise in my soul. She is very sensitive to the needs and disadvantages of the very poor.

Sylvia, one of her other daughters, has lived and worked in the East End, among working-class women, for many years. She knows the dire necessity for women's rights there. I am very inspired by her.

George Lansbury, one of our greatest advocates, has been thrown out of the Labour Party because of his support for women's suffrage. He is going to stand as an independent candidate, fighting his seat on the issue of women's suffrage, sponsored by us. This is really exciting and it takes the Cause very much in the direction that I have dreamed of.

My mother and all my brothers and their wives attended this evening's meeting. I know they don't all agree, but at least they showed up. And my mother is sympathetic. Well, sometimes. She got agitated when she heard Mrs Pankhurst's call to militancy.

I feel hope and enthusiasm again.

8th December 1912

Suffragettes have been attacking letter-boxes, burning letters, setting off false fire alarms. There have been more arrests, including dear Miss Baker, who has barely been out of prison this year. Flora wants to know where I am at every minute of the day. I will not even write in this diary what I have been involved in because I fear she may find it and read it. Not that she ever has intruded on my privacy in the past, but she is worried about my safety.

The government and members of the public are beginning to view Mrs Pankhurst as a dangerous revolutionary. Plain-clothes policemen are attending all our meetings, taking notes of everything that is said. It is all so ridiculous. Why don't they just give women the vote?

16th December 1912

Mr Asquith has told the House today that the Manhood Suffrage Bill will have its second reading after Christmas.

Millicent Fawcett is pressurizing us to halt all aggressive activities until we see whether there will be women's suffrage amendments included in the bill. I bet there won't be. Why would Mr Asquith give us changes this time when he has broken his word countless times in the past?

10th January 1913

I received a letter in the post from Mrs Pankhurst. It has been sent to all members of the WSPU. It states that it is our obligation to stand up for our rights through militant acts:

...If any woman refrains from militant protest against the injury done by the government and the House of Commons to women and to the race, she will share the responsibility of the crime...

The letter goes on to request an acknowledgement of our support. Obviously, she has mine. But I have hidden the letter at the very bottom of my chest of drawers.

27th January 1913

Asquith's government introduced its Manhood Suffrage Bill today, but when it reached the floor the Speaker of the House of Commons would not permit any changes. He ruled that to include women's suffrage amendments would so alter the nature of the Bill that a whole new one would need to be introduced. So it was decided to drop the Manhood Suffrage Bill for this session!

Emmeline was furious. She says that no one can ever again believe Mr Asquith to be a man of honour. I have never seen her so mad.

28th January 1913

I threw stones in Whitehall today as a protest and broke several windows. I was not arrested but 49 others were.

15th February 1913

A house that was being constructed for David Lloyd George has been seriously damaged in a fire by some of our women. Emmeline has been arrested, although she was nowhere near the scene of the crime. I doubt the authorities believe she is personally guilty of the deed, but she has been charged with incitement to commit a felony.

18th February 1913

Asquith's decision has caused a chain of destructive acts. Hordes of women are going to extremes now to win the vote, and society is expressing its shock at our "delinquent" behaviour. But what will it take to make the government listen?

Perhaps Emily Wilding Davison was right when

she told me that the Cause needs someone to die for it. Not me, though. I am definitely not brave enough.

4th March 1913

The news today is that cricket pavilions, racecourse stands and golf clubhouses have been set on fire. Many women have been arrested, including *me*. I have to confess that now the moment has come, I am petrified. Flora begged to pay my fine, but I wouldn't agree. I will serve my sentence and play my part.

She has promised to notify Mother. If she doesn't hear from me, she will worry.

5th March 1913

Mrs Pankhurst has been sentenced to THREE years' penal servitude for the destruction of the Chancellor of the Exchequer's future home.

I have been imprisoned in Holloway in the Second Division. There are 81 of us in here. Some have been given terms of up to six months. My sentence is two months. I shall protest at my status as a non-political prisoner. I am on hunger strike.

17th March 1913

I am weak today; my writing is shaky. I have little strength, though I am determined to keep a record of every day that passes in this stinking place.

19th March 1913

This morning, when my turn came to be force-fed, I had intended to be resistant and beat off the prison staff, but I am weak and I was shaking with fear, and I failed miserably. Four big wardresses came into my cell, wrapped a towel around me and without further ado pinned me down against the bunk. One of them clamped her hand over my mouth and squeezed it closed. Then a doctor arrived. He was carrying all manner of horrific-looking equipment. He proceeded to insert a rubber tube of approximately two feet in length up my left nostril. It was horrendous. At first I had a tickling sensation and then my eyes began to sting. Then he threaded it further and further until it was fed down my throat. My eyes were weeping. I was gasping for breath and fighting the women, who were too strong for me. A china funnel was then attached to the other end of the piping and a mushy, cabbage-like liquid was poured into it. The doctor took my pulse while one of the wardresses pinched closed my right nostril. Now both were blocked and I couldn't breathe at all. I thought that I would suffocate or choke to death. My eyes were streaming and my arms and shoulders ached from the force of being pinned against my bunk. I fought for breath until the liquid was sucked up into my nose and down my throat, which is the point of this horrid, cruel exercise.

A basin of water was then placed in front of me and the tube was withdrawn and put into the basin. Mucous and phlegm came out with it. I kept spitting as though something was still stuck inside me. My chest throbbed with pain and I felt sick and very dizzy.

I have been at Union meetings where they have discussed the barbarity of this treatment. I remember the letter Marion Dunlop Wallace read out to us all; I have friends who have been through it, but nothing, NOTHING, prepares you for the horror and indignity of experiencing it.

What is even worse is that the tubes they are using are not sterilized. Force-feeding the insane in hospitals is only carried out if it is to save life. Here, it is an act of violence and could very possibly cause serious infection, or if the liquid passes into the lungs it could cause pneumonia.

20th March 1913

I have spent three days, not consecutively, in solitary confinement for hitting one of the wardresses when she forced me against my bunk. Books have been forbidden me. On the days when I have been locked in solitary, I have been allowed no breaks for exercise. Those days are the worst. It is *so* lonely. Twice I have ended up in tears. One of the other problems is that I am so cut off from the Cause, from the news of what is happening.

I have served a fortnight of my time. Fifteen days: it feels like fifteen years.

13th April 1913

The whisper within the prison is that Emmeline is very sick. She collapses frequently. They are not force-feeding her but she is on hunger strike and has been surviving on nothing but water.

I think the Governors are worried that she might die. Lena, another suffragette in here, says they fear that her death would make a martyr of her. There is talk of releasing her until she recovers her health and then hauling her back in again to complete her sentence. I wept when I heard this, and because I am so tired and weak myself. My legs are growing wobbly.

The only way I can calculate the date is by marking off each day as it passes. As I write, the letters swim about in front of my eyes. I am scared that my notes will be found so I hide them in my underwear. I am writing on scruffy bits of paper intended to be used for hygiene purposes.

I have now served over a month. Some of my hair is beginning to fall out and my teeth feel funny. I shake a lot and am always dizzy. I rarely move from my bunk.

25th April 1913

The government is so determined that Emmeline Pankhurst and others like her should not attempt another hunger strike and thus find themselves released from prison without having served their full sentence, or die inside and become martyrs, that it has introduced a new act. Its official title is The Prisoners' Temporary Discharge of Ill Health Act.

The idea is that if our women go on hunger strike they will no longer be stopped, nor will they be force-fed, but in order that they do not die in prison and so become martyrs, as soon as they grow seriously weak they will be discharged from prison. If they die outside, the law does not give two hoots, but if they survive, the moment they are recovered and have strength, they will be arrested again and obliged to continue their sentence.

It has been nicknamed the Cat-and-Mouse Act. The police are the cats and we are the mice, it seems.

I have ten days left of my sentence to serve. Some days I feel that I won't make it. For the past three days, since they stopped force-feeding me, I have had nothing but water. I feel sick, then retch but there is nothing in my system to throw up.

5th May 1913

Freedom. I thought I would jump for joy but I can barely walk. I am so weak I felt blinded by the light and noise when I shuffled out of those gates today. Flora and Mother were waiting there with Flora's car. They were anxious but thrilled to see me. Both tried to behave as though everything was normal. When Mother embraced me, she wept loudly. They wanted to take me for a meal but I could not have swallowed a mouthful. Instead, we drove back to Bloomsbury in Flora's Fiat and they put me to bed.

What a treat to have Mother with me, at Flora's. I felt safe and happy.

6th May 1913

I have slept for sixteen hours. When I woke Mother was at my side.

"You're a stubborn one you are, Dollie, just like me. But you're brave, too, and I admire you for what you've done."

I think those words mattered to me more than anything.

20th May 1913

My health is improving. I have put on some weight but my moods are dark. I am haunted by the memory of the cries from the neighbouring cells. Women in pain, women giving birth, women being force-fed. Women petrified.

4th June 1913

Derby Day. Epsom racecourse. Not only is this horse race one of the most important events in the English calendar, it is also a day of great social importance. The elite of British society attends this meeting, including the King and Queen with a host of guests.

What a far cry it will be from Holloway prison! I am attending because I have learned a secret. There is to be some form of protest, but I don't know what it will be. I am not involved. Flora is driving down with me. I have not told her why I want to be there, but she is happy to indulge me in this outing

I shall write more later.

Later

My God, what a shocking day.

The crowds attending were numerous indeed. And what finery! I have rarely seen such outfits. It was like a scene dreamed up for a moving-picture show.

Epsom is shaped almost like a horse-shoe. The races are flat sprints. At one of the events, the King entered into competition a horse named Anmer, and the crowds flocked to the railings to watch it perform. Flora and I were positioned close to the finishing line.

The start took the jockeys along a fast straight that led to a long and gradual bend. The bend sharpened at Tattenham Corner, where the horses slowed down before picking up into the home straight to finish in front of the Royal Box.

As they drew towards us, the horses were galloping for their lives, battling it out towards those final furlongs. It was terribly exciting. I was jumping up and down, entirely caught up in the thrilling atmosphere: thudding hooves; fresh, sharp air; crowds shouting for the King's horse or for whichever animal they had placed their bets on. And then, suddenly, a small figure, a woman, appeared on the track. She had slipped beneath the iron railing and was pounding towards the approaching beasts. A flash of material caught my attention. White, green and purple. Our colours! Inside her coat she had sewn the suffragettes' flag. She ran like lightning towards the galloping horses and, as Anmer rounded the very last bend at Tattenham Corner, she grabbed – Lord knows how – the King's horse by its bridle.

"It's one of them women!" "What does she think she's doing?" Questions, voices, catcalls were being hurled from every direction.

"Who is that?" begged Flora. "I can't make out her face."

By then I knew exactly who it was.

Emily Wilding Davison.

"Emily, stop!" I screamed, fearing she would break her back.

The speed of the charging horses sent her flying. She actually somersaulted. It was the most extraordinary and terrifying sight.

I went cold, remembering what she had spoken of in the past.

The crowd roared and shouted. Folk were appalled. The jockey was thrown. He went flying like a bullet through the air. The horse went down, stumbling and neighing, and there on the ground stretched out before the beast lay Emily, my comrade. A heavy silence settled, as though the world was in shock, but then people began to swarm out of the throng, from behind the white-painted rails, on to the racecourse itself. There was much shouting and calling of orders. Confusion and panic took the place of the earlier competition excitement. I looked about for our bearded King George V or his wife, Queen Mary, but, although they were there somewhere, neither came forward. Lord knows what the King was thinking. Of his poor animal, I suppose. Eventually, the horse managed to stagger to its feet, but clearly it was traumatized. The jockey also got up, but not Emily. Her injuries were far too grave.

"Did you know about this?" Flora asked me.

I shook my head.

9th June 1913

Emily died yesterday afternoon. She was operated on last Friday but her condition never really improved. Mary Leigh, Charlie Marsh and several other close suffrage friends visited her bedside. Flora tells me that someone had draped the WSPU colours from the screen around her bed.

She has become the first martyr to our movement, prepared to give her life for women's rights, for what she passionately believed in, but what a horrible shock to us all!

I want to say a word or two about Emily because there are many now who are calling her crazy, or a "crank" or hysterical, particularly the newspapers and the establishment, who take every opportunity to ridicule our cause. Others are accusing her of doing more damage than good, but these remarks, all of them, are unjust.

Emily studied at Oxford University where she gained a first-class honours degree. Well, that is to say, she sat the exams, but because she was a woman she was not entitled to actually claim the degree or use it professionally. Later, she went on to London University, where she took a BA. London University is less stuffy than Oxford and they allowed her the honour.

From this it is clear that she was hardworking and determined. Emily was not a crazy crank or a fanatic, but a passionate woman and a serious-minded, sensitive individual who cared desperately that a woman's place in society should be equal to that of a man. So strong was her commitment that she believed the Cause was worth dying for if, in the dying, she could bring our fight closer to resolution.

21st June 1913

Emily's coffin, draped in our colours, was followed by 2,000 uniformed suffragettes. Charlie Marsh – she and I broke windows together in the Strand – carried a cross. Flora and I walked side by side, holding hands, sisters in silence. My mother accompanied us, too. It was very moving.

The coffin was placed on a train at King's Cross Station, headed for its final resting place in Northumberland. Many women accompanied it, keeping vigil by it. Bizarrely, I glimpsed, among the throng of faces, Celia Loverton. I called and called, but there was no way I could have reached her or caught her attention. Still, it satisfied me enormously to see her there. The word is spreading. Women everywhere are understanding that this is their battle, whoever they are, whatever their background.

Emily was buried near her home in Morpeth. It is intended that her gravestone will be inscribed, "Deeds not Words".

I think many of us are left with dozens of questions and a sense of emptiness. I know that I am.

I shall end this diary now. I began it to be my companion after the loss of Lady Violet. I have found friends and, I believe, my path in life. Now my energies must be directed towards the future: gaining a place at university and afterwards finding work as a journalist so that I can tell our suffrage story, which, by then, I trust will have a triumphant ending.

Emily is dead. Thousands of us have served some time in prisons all over Great Britain, manhandled and despised. For what? Because we believe that we are the equal of men, that we have the right to participate in the building of a just and equal society and because we cannot stand silently looking on while almost 50 per cent of British people live in conditions that are below the breadline, conditions that force them to scratch and scrape a living, in what is nothing short of an abyss.

We act with courage, proud to be women.

And so our fight goes on.

Historical Note

Calls for women's rights date back many years. One of the earliest was *Vindication of the Rights of Women* published by Mary Wollstonecraft in 1792. Some individual women called for the vote during the 1830s and 1840s. However, organized campaigning did not get underway until the 1860s.

Women were not allowed in the House of Commons. Instead they relied on sympathetic MPs to present their case. In 1866 a Second Reform Bill was being debated. Emily Davies and Elizabeth Garrett presented a petition to JS Mill, MP for Westminster and a supporter of women's rights. Mill presented the petition to the House of Commons, asking for suitably qualified women to be included in the Bill. MPs voted the demand out by 194 votes to 73. Working-class men in towns gained the vote, but women were excluded.

In 1866 a woman called Lydia Becker formed the Manchester Women's Suffrage Society; other societies were set up in London and Edinburgh. Relying on friends in the House, Lydia Becker and other women presented petitions to Parliament every year. All were rejected.

At this point, many people were opposed to giving women the vote. The arguments varied. Many people believed a woman's place was in the home and that it was against nature for women to be involved in politics; a man's world. Others believed men were superior to women and therefore politics should be left to them.

In 1884 the right to vote was extended to working-class men in rural areas. Again women were excluded. By this stage they had won the right to work as nurses, teachers, factory workers and could own property, but still they were not entitled to vote.

Women in New Zealand gained the vote in 1893 and a year later the vote was given to women in South Australia. In 1895 the British general election returned a number of MPs sympathetic to women's suffrage.

Encouraged by these events, the women's suffrage campaign gained momentum and the women's fight for the vote became a major political issue. Thousands of women up and down the country rallied to "the Cause", as it became known.

There were two main strands. The first and largest organization was the The National Union of Women's

Suffrage Societies (NUWSS). Formed in 1897 under the leadership of Mrs Millicent Fawcett, it brought together all the existing women's suffrage societies. The NUWSS was run on democratic lines and believed in using only peaceful methods to win the vote. By 1914 it had a membership of nearly 60,000 women throughout the country. They were known as suffragists from the word suffrage meaning the right to vote.

The second strand was the Women's Social and Political Union (WSPU). It was formed in 1903 in Manchester by Emmeline Pankhurst and her two daughters, Christabel, a law student, and Sylvia, a socialist and artist. The aim of the WSPU was immediate enfranchisement. From the outset, the WSPU rejected traditional campaigning in favour of militant action. From 1906 its members became known as suffragettes, to distinguish them from the law-abiding suffragists.

As time passed, WSPU tactics became increasingly militant. Between 1906 and 1914 more than 1,000 women were arrested and went to prison. From 1909 many imprisoned suffragettes went on hunger strike. The government introduced force-feeding, a brutal technique, which caused a public outcry and won the suffragettes enormous support. However, not all women agreed with the militant tactics of the WSPU. While the Pankhursts and their followers rushed the Houses of Parliament, the NUWSS continued to petition peacefully and educate the public through pamphlets and books.

Despite their differences the two organizations often worked together, joining forces at huge demonstrations and meetings. By 1910 it looked as if success might be in sight. The newly formed Labour Party supported votes for women, although they were uncertain about how it should be achieved. Some Liberals, too, supported the woman's vote, although their leader, Asquith, and other powerful men in the party, were determinedly opposed. An all-party committee in the House of Commons drew up a conciliation bill, which would have given votes to women householders and wives of male householders but, largely due to the manoeuverings of Prime Minister Asquith, it was defeated.

This infuriated the WSPU. From 1911 suffragettes turned to ever more militant tactics. In 1912 they broke hundreds of windows in London's West End. The leadership was arrested except for Christabel, who fled to France.

Over the following few years, suffragettes carried out a series of arson attacks on houses, railway stations and other buildings. No one was hurt but these tactics alienated the British public.

In 1914, World War I broke out. Emmeline and Christabel called an end to their militant campaign. They threw their energies behind the war effort, working with the government to recruit soldiers and women workers. This did not please all members of the WSPU. The organization split. Some women, including Sylvia Pankhurst, joined the peace movement, others continued to work for suffrage peacefully. By 1917 the WSPU no longer existed. Suffragettes were released from prison and thousands of British women were recruited into the war effort. They worked in all areas from munitions factories to nursing on the Western Front. It was increasingly clear that women could no longer be excluded from voting. In 1918 the Electoral Reform Bill finally gave the vote to all house-holding women aged 30 and over. A second Act allowed women over 21 to become MPs. Seventeen women stood for Parliament, including Christabel Pankhurst but only one was elected and she did not take her seat.

In 1919, during a by-election, Viscountess Nancy Astor became the first female MP in the House of Commons. By 1923 there were eight women in Parliament. In 1928 the vote was extended to women aged 21 and over, on equal terms with men.

Timeline

1866 Women's Suffrage Societies founded in London, Manchester and later Edinburgh.

1869 House-owning women gain the right to vote in local elections.

1871–1883 Private members' bills for women's suffrage are presented to every year without success.

1897 National Union of Women's Suffrage Societies (NUWSS) formed, with Millicent Fawcett as president.

1903 Pankhursts and others launch the Women's Suffrage and Political Union (WSPU) in Manchester. They break away from traditional campaigning methods used by previous societies.

1905 Christabel Pankhurst and Annie Kenney are arrested outside the Free Trade Hall. Votes for Women becomes headline news.

1906 October: Ten WSPU members are arrested outside the House of Commons.

1907 WSPU publish their newspaper, *Votes for Women*.

1909 Marjorie Wallace Dunlop becomes the first suffragette to go on hunger strike.

1909 Conciliation Committee formed to draft a woman's suffrage bill (the Conciliation Bill). WSPU calls a truce. Between 1910 and 1912 three bills are drafted and debated. All are defeated.

1910 Black Friday: police assault women following a rush on the House of Commons.

1911 WSPU become increasingly militant following the failure of the Conciliation Bill.

1912 Police raid WSPU headquarters and arrest the leadership. Christabel escapes to France.

1913 April: The Prisoner's Temporary Discharge for Ill-Health Act, nicknamed the Cat-and-Mouse Act is rushed through Parliament.

1913 June: Suffragette Emily Wilding Davison dies from injuries.

1918 The Representation of the People Act gives the vote to all women over 30 who are householders or wives of householders; occupiers of property with an annual rent of £45 or over and graduates of British universities. These changes give more than 8.4 million British women the right to vote.

1928 All women over 21 gain the vote, irrespective of property qualifications.

Emmeline and Christabel Pankhurst, founders and leaders of the WSPU.

Emmeline Pethwick-Lawrence, one of the leaders of the WSPU until 1912.

A suffragette selling Votes for Women. *The sellers had to stand in the road otherwise the police might charge them with obstruction.*

Millicent Garrett Fawcett, the President of the NUWSS, speaking at a march in Hyde Park, London.

A WSPU membership card designed by Mrs Pankhurst.

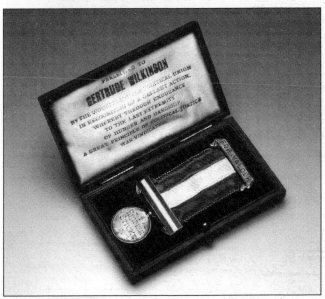

A WSPU medal. This medal was awarded to members of the WSPU who went on hunger strike while in prison.

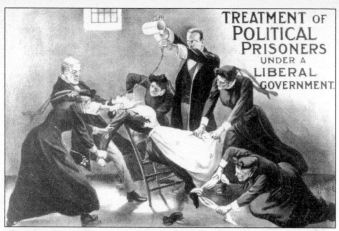

This political poster shows the brutal practice of force-feeding women in prison.

Picture acknowledgments

P 220 (top)   Emmeline and Christabel Pankhurst, Mary Evans/
The Women's Library

P 220 (bottom)   Emmeline Pethwick-Lawrence, Mary Evans/The
Women's Library

P 221   Selling *Votes for Women*, Mary Evans/The Women's
Library

P 222   Millicent Garrett Fawcett, Mary Evans/The Women's
Library

P 223 (top)   WSPU card, Mary Evans/The Women's Library

P 223 (bottom)   Hunger strike medal, Mary Evans/The Women's Library

P 224   Force-feeding poster, Mary Evans Picture Library